M000189885

WWW.BEWAREORMONSTERS.COM

PRAISE FOR JEREMY ROBINSON

"[*Hunger* is] a wicked step-child of King and Del Toro. Lock your windows and bolt your doors. [Robinson, writing as] Jeremiah Knight, imagines the post-apocalypse like no one else."

—The Novel Blog

"Robinson writes compelling thrillers, made all the more entertaining by the way he incorporates aspects of pop culture into the action."

—Booklist

"*Project 731* is a must. Jeremy Robinson just keeps getting better with every new adventure and monster he creates."

—Suspense Magazine

"Robinson is known for his great thrillers, and [with *XOM-B*] he has written a novel that will be in contention for various science fiction awards at the end of the year. Robinson continues to amaze with his active imagination."

—Booklist

"Robinson puts his distinctive mark on Michael Crichton territory with [*Island 731*], a terrifying present-day riff on *The Island of Dr. Moreau*. Action and scientific explanation are appropriately proportioned, making this one of the best *Jurassic Park* successors."

—Publisher's Weekly
Starred Review

"[Jeremy Robinson's *SecondWorld* is] a brisk thriller with neatly timed action sequences, snappy dialogue and the ultimate sympathetic figure in a badly burned little girl with a fighting spirit... The Nazis are determined to have the last gruesome laugh in this efficient doomsday thriller."

—Kirkus Reviews

"Jeremy Robinson is the next James Rollins."

—Chris Kuzneski,
NY Times bestselling author of
The Einstein Pursuit

PRAISE FOR J. KENT HOLLOWAY

"Not since Preston & Child's Agent Pendergast has there been a more mysterious, charming and fun to read sleuth as Ezekiel Crane. His mixture of southern charm, dark history and scientific know-how is intoxicating."

—Jeremy Robinson,
international bestselling author of
Project Nemesis

"Holloway skillfully weaves a back-woods tapestry of Sherlock Holmes with TV's *Supernatural* and *Justified* into a thrilling Appalachian story of magic and mayhem. The Dirge amps up the action, menace, and mojo, for a spookfest of epic proportions, with a layered mystery and surprises at every turn. Join Ezekiel Crane, and bring your ten-demon bag for another Dark Hollows adventure. This series somehow got even better."

—Kane Gilmour,
international bestselling author of
The Crypt of Dracula

"*Siren's Song* hits all the right notes. A page-turning plot, heart-stopping battles above and below the waves, cutting-edge technology and weaponry — and of course, more double-crossing villains than you can shake a spear-gun at. Holloway's a skilled conductor, and *Siren's Song* a thrilling symphony."

—David Sakmyster,
international bestselling author of
The Pharos Objective

"Killer mermaids, government conspiracies, and women as beautiful as they are evil. Sirens' Song will lure you to the last page!"

—Rick Chesler,
international bestselling author of
Wired Kingdom

PATRIOT

A JACK SIGLER CONTINUUM NOVELLA

JEREMY ROBINSON

WITH J. KENT HOLLOWAY

BREAKNECK MEDIA

Visit Jeremy Robinson on the World Wide Web at:
www.bewareofmonsters.com

Visit J. Kent Holloway on the World Wide Web at:
www.kenthollowayonline.com

ALSO BY JEREMY ROBINSON

ALSO BY J. KENT HOLLOWAY

The Jack Sigler Continuum Series
Guardian
Patriot
Centurion (2016)

The ENIGMA Directive Series
Primal Thirst
Sirens' Song
Devil's Child

The Dark Hollows Mystery Series
The Curse of One-Eyed Jack
The Dirge of Briaresnare Marsh

The Legend of the Winterking
The Crown of Nandur

The Knightshade Legacy Series
The Djinn

Short Stories
"Freakshow" (An ENIGMA Directive Short Story)
"Masquerade at One Thousand Feet"
"Haunted Melody" (A Meikle Bay Horror Short Story)

PATRIOT

A JACK SIGLER CONTINUUM NOVELLA

J. Kent Holloway would like to dedicate this book to:

*"...my amazing co-workers and friends at the District 23
Medical Examiner's office.
Thank you for your unending patience with me, as I continue
my dream of writing.
You guys continue to amaze me."*

THE CONTINUUM SERIES

Jack Sigler: A Man Out of Time

Jack Sigler was a modern soldier. First for the Army, then for the anti-terror Delta unit known as 'Chess Team' and finally for Endgame, a black budget organization specializing in fending off strange and otherworldly global threats. After several brutal, yet successful missions, the man known by the callsign: King, found himself torn away from his family and thrust back in time, abandoned in the year 780 BC. But that's not where his life would end. He was gifted with regenerative powers, making him nearly immortal. He heals quickly. Doesn't age. And he was nearly 2800 years away from his daughter and fiancée.

Now, the only way he can return to his own time and his family is to live, fight and sometimes wage war through the oncoming centuries, carrying on Endgame's mission: to protect the weak, right wrongs and send the world's monsters back to whatever hell spawned them.

Patriot, the second tale in the *Jack Sigler Continuum* series, takes place after King has lived in the past for over twenty-five hundred years...

1

Kavo Zile
The British Caribbean Islands, 1775

Quartermaster John Greer's lungs heaved, straining to draw in enough air to continue trudging through the waist-high, algae-filmed water. His boots, already thick with the caked-on jungle muck, felt like lead. He sloshed his way past a forest of cattails, bramble and gnarled trees that grasped at his clothing, as if the land itself was famished for human flesh. Despite the malevolent terrain, however, Greer couldn't help but feel as though there was something much worse lurking somewhere in the dense jungle. Although neither he, nor his crew, had encountered any signs of life greater than the occasional bird or bird-sized flying insect, his nerves were edged as sharp as a cutlass.

When he reached the swamp's shoreline, Greer stopped. He glanced back at the others as they slowly closed the distance toward him. As the second-in-command of the Continental privateer vessel, the *Reardon's Mark*, Greer was appalled at the decrepit condition of his crew. Though he, too, was approaching near exhaustion from the half a day's march they'd made into the Caribbean island's interior, the others appeared almost ready to collapse.

This will never do, he thought. *Not at all.*

The *Mark*'s captain, Josiah Reardon, would have never tolerated such lack of discipline in their old Royal Navy days, and Greer was determined to whip his men back into shape, just as soon as they had claimed what they'd come to retrieve from this accursed island.

Catching his breath, he waited for the men to reach him, and rolled his eyes as the crew parted to make way for the short, rotund man wheezing his way to the front of the group. Greer had experienced an automatic distaste for the older man from the moment they'd met, three weeks before, and his ire had only grown since. The man, Jim Brannan Finkle, was some kind of scientist, and he had commissioned the *Reardon's Mark* crew on orders from General Washington. For most of the men, this was reason enough to hold the old man in a state of near worshipping awe, but Greer—being part of the Continental Navy only by happenstance of a slight misunderstanding between himself and a Royal Admiral's wife—had never held George Washington in great esteem.

"I say, Greer," the scientist said, waddling up to the quartermaster while wiping away a stream of sweat from his prodigious forehead. "I could use a few minutes to catch both my breath and my bearings."

Greer nodded, and allowed his men to rest, while Finkle fumbled through his leather messenger bag for a tattered waxen map he kept folded among his belongings.

"I know it's in here somewhere," Finkle said, mumbling to himself while pushing his spectacles further onto the hump of his nose. "Ah! Here it is." With a dramatic flourish, the scientist whipped the map out, unfolded it and placed it carefully on a decaying tree stump to his right. Greer watched silently as the old busybody scanned the yellowing map, and he jerked nervously when Finkle burst out with an excited, "Ha!"

"What? What did you find?"

Finkle looked up at the officer, and a smile began to stretch slowly across his face. "According to this, we're only about five miles from the boneyard. We should make it there well before sundown."

"And are you finally going to tell me what you hope to find, once we come to this obviously heathen cemetery?"

Finkle looked up from the map, and eyed him curiously. He then shrugged the question away, and continued to study the map. "What I don't understand is this... The legend says that *Lanme Wa*'s cursed pirate crew guards this island, yet we've not seen hide nor hair of any living soul."

"Lanme Wa?"

The old man folded the map, and stuffed it back into his bag before pulling his long graying hair back, and tying it into a pony tail. He then nodded. "Lanme Wa. A famous pirate around the turn of the century. He's said to reside within the boneyard."

"From the turn of the century? We're looking for the tomb of a pirate that's been dead since the turn of the century, and you honestly expect to run into his crew?"

"You know, they say Lanme Wa once had a heated battle with Ed Thatch...um, Blackbeard...and won. Quite impressive." Finkle chuckled, seemingly oblivious to the quartermaster's dismay. "And I never said the pirate was *dead*. I simply said he's supposed to reside within the boneyard. There's a difference."

Greer stared silently at Finkle for several long seconds, before shaking his head, and shouting at his men. "Nichols! Spratt! Front and center!" A moment later, the two beckoned crewmen hustled up to him with stiff salutes.

"Aye, Mr. Greer," Nichols said, still saluting, which wasn't necessary. As quartermaster of a pirate, or privateer crew, he was second-in-command of the vessel on which they sailed. But the difference between pirates and the Royal Navy was that each of the men in a pirate crew were considered equal partners. Captains and quartermasters were voted into their positions. And they could be voted out, as well. But like Reardon and Greer, Nichols hailed from Royal Navy stock, and old habits could certainly be difficult to overcome.

Nichols was lean, almost emaciated, and he had an empty socket where one of his eyes had been stabbed with a pen knife, during a card game three years before. He was also the ship's cook, and he had an exceptional gift for turning even worm-infested potatoes into the most exquisite delicacies.

"I need you and Spratt to scout ahead," Greer said. "We're drawing closer to our destination, and I find this expedition of ours to be unnervingly uneventful. If we're walking into some type of trap, I'd like to know in advance."

Nichols and Spratt glanced nervously at one another, but snapped off another salute, and bounded deeper into the jungle. Once they were no longer visible, Greer turned back to Finkle. It was time to get the answers he'd wanted since their longboats had arrived on Kavo Zile—a Haitian name that meant 'Island of the Grave.' "Tell me, who exactly was this Lanme Wa fellow? I've not heard of him before."

Finkle, now relaxing on the stump, and taking a leisurely pull on his long-stemmed pipe, eyed the quarter-master. There a gleam in the old man's eyes that seemed magnified by the thick glass of his strange looking spectacles. After expelling a plume of gray smoke, he sighed. "I suppose it can't hurt to tell you a little about him, though

I'm still not permitted to tell you everything I've learned of the man," he said. "You already know of the mission General Washington has sent us on. I believe Lanme Wa is the key to its success."

Greer sat down on the ground, crossing his legs in Indian fashion, and he swatted at a mosquito that alighted on his neck. Even sitting on the ground, his eyes were level with the shorter scientist. "You're going to have to explain that, sir."

Finkle nodded. "Lanme Wa has gone by a few names in the past. But it wasn't until he and his pirate crew took a slaver ship sailing into Charles Town around 1663 that he was given that name." Taking a tamper, he packed down the tobacco in the pipe bowl down, and relit it. "It's Creole, and means 'Sea King.' Story goes that upon freeing the slaves, he took them to a port on a beautiful tropical island, off any map. He set them up, and ensured that a supply ship would visit the island every six months, to see to any needs they might have."

"How very un-pirate-like."

"Quite. But the slaves revered him for the freedom he had granted, and they gave him the name Lanme Wa to show their eternal gratitude toward him. They elevated him to almost god-like reverence, as a matter of fact...which is all the more odd considering the descriptions they gave of his crew."

"All right. Color me intrigued," Greer said. "What did they say about his crew?"

"That they were damned. Cursed," Finkle said, a single eyebrow raising high against his forehead. "Said they were creatures black as pitch—which is quite something given the race of those making the claims—and that they would only sail at night. Never by day."

"That's hardly proof that this crew was damned."

"They also had strange hungers, very difficult to sate. The most impressive bit is that they, like their master, could not be killed."

"Oh, come now, Finkle," Greer said. "You are supposed to be a man of science! Would you have me believe such ghost stories?"

Finkle laughed. "Your Britishness is betraying you, sir. Remember, as the Bard once said, 'there are more things in heaven and earth'...et cetera, et cetera. But as I was saying..."

The sound of a twig snapping to their left wheeled Greer and his crew around. Muskets and flintlock pistols shot up, pointing in the direction of the noise. The quartermaster, now on his feet and peering into the overgrowth, eased the hammer of his pistol back. "Hello? Nichols? Spratt? Is that you?"

Another snap sounded in the opposite direction, spinning each man around again. This time, however, Greer noticed old Finkle was brandishing his own pistol as well.

"Master Greer," came a deep voice, from the direction of his crew.

Greer glanced over at them to see a large, bare-chested black man stepping out from behind his men. His head was shaved clean, but his cheeks and chin were flecked with dark patches of hair. Several scars and tattooed dots covered the man's face from forehead to cheeks, which marked the tribe from which he'd come. If Greer remembered correctly, the man's name was William. He was the ship's purser, and the personal slave to Captain Reardon.

"What is it, William?" Greer had already turned his gaze back to the jungle.

"We need caution in dis place," William said, his baritone voice rumbling like a roll of thunder. "Da *l'wa* are about. Dis land is sacred to dem, and whites ain't always welcome amongst dem."

What in Jehovah's creation is this simpleton going on about?

Greer stifled an impulse to berate the purser for his ridiculously superstitious warning. Of course, no one could be a sailor in the New World or have any dealings with the African slaves without having heard of their heathen fantasies. The l'wa, or loa as the English called them, were supposedly spiritual beings that served a greater god of some kind. Depending on the family the loa belonged to, these spirits were either kind or harsh. Brutal even. Greer had seen his fair share of sailors—both legitimate and pirate—succumb to the island superstitions over the years. They took up the practice of Vodou to better their lot in life, or at least to protect themselves from harm on the high seas. However, among his crew, there would be no such nonsense. Greer decided to reprimand William later, once they'd returned to the *Mark*.

Gesturing for the man to stay silent, Greer concentrated on locating what had snapped the twig. Taking another step toward the vegetation, he leaned forward. A round yellow object burst out of the jungle's interior, narrowly missing Greer's head. He whipped around, tracking the projectile, until it rolled to a stop three feet away.

Some type of fruit, he thought, stooping to pick up the oblong object. He recognized it as what some local tribes in these parts called the paw-paw. *Papaya.*

William hissed, then spat on the ground at the sight of the fruit. "I tell you...da l'wa are angry, and dey warn you now. Dis is Grave Island, home of da *Ghede* l'wa. Spirits of da dead."

"William!" Greer snapped. "You will remain silent, or you will be flogged." To show his disdain for the superstitious drivel, the quartermaster bit into the sweetly sour fruit, and savored the taste. He then grinned broadly at the slave to reinforce the message.

"It's a shame," came a soft, feminine voice behind him. He twisted around to see a stunning black woman, standing barefoot and wearing a light cotton shift, scandalously see-through, which left her shoulders and legs bare. From her lighter complexion and soft facial features, Greer recognized her instantly as Creole. Her dark black hair exploded in all directions, reminding him of a black lion's mane. Her emerald green eyes seemed to glimmer in the twilight. Nichols and Spratt stood on either side of her, their muskets ready. "You really should listen to Master William, *mon cher.* I dare say, he be wiser dan any of you."

"Nichols, who, pray tell, is this?" Greer shouted, completely baffled by the presence of a lone female upon the uninhabited island.

But she continued before the cook could respond to the question. "A word o' warning, gentlemen. When you come to da boneyard, you'll be wantin' to beware da *Brave Ghede.* He not be likin' da livin' amongst da dead." She then laughed, winked at Greer and folded her arms across her chest defiantly. "But if you like, I'll take you to see Lanme Wa right now. Makes no nevermind to me."

2

With Nichols and Spratt still leveling their weapons at the Creole woman, Greer and the expedition had continued their trek further into the island's interior. Fascinated, Finkle walked in step with her, barraging her with questions concerning her origins and her purpose upon the island.

"I am a *mambo bokor* of vodou," she said with a laugh, the sound of rainwater against a window pane. "I serve da l'wa, just as my mothers and grandmothers did from before I was born. It was da l'wa who brought me here, to serve da house of da Ghede...da l'wa of da Dead."

"Fascinating," Finkle cooed, eyeing the feminine bokor. "Absolutely fascinating. So tell me..."

"I want to know if it was you who threw that paw-paw fruit at me earlier," Greer said, catching up to them. "It nearly took my head off."

The mambo bokor glanced over at him, her smile stretching coyly up one side of her face. "A paw-paw fruit? Here? On Kavo Zile?"

"That's what I said. A paw-paw was hurled only seconds before you appeared. If it was you, I'll see that you answer for your insolence."

"John, come now," Finkle said. "Don't be rude to our gracious hostess."

"I'm an officer of the Continental Navy." It wasn't entirely true. A quartermaster wasn't considered an officer in the same way as his lieutenant rank while he had been in the Royal Navy. But he knew no one would argue the point. "And I am deserving of a modicum of respect, whether I'm in the official fleet, or on a privateer's vessel. She *will* answer the question."

"Sir?" The voice came from behind them, and belonged to Nichols. "Beggin' yer pardon, but it couldn't 'ave been her. We found her during our scout, and she was with us until we returned, just after the paw-paw incident. We'd'a seen her throw it."

"Besides," the bokor added, "dere are no paw-paw trees on dis island. Dey do not grow here."

Greer stopped walking, causing Spratt to nearly march into the back of him. The quartermaster recovered quickly, and jogged to catch up to the woman and Finkle. "I know what I saw. I tasted it. It was papaya. I have no doubt."

"And I do not doubt you, *cher*," she said with a giggle. "Da l'wa are crafty in deir mischief, and not limited to any one locale. You doubt deir existence, so dey merely wanted to convince you." She held up a hand, bringing the entire company to a halt. "We are almost dere." She turned around to face Greer and the others. "We are about to enter a most holy site. Da *Simityè Dyab la.*"

Greer glanced at Finkle, who shrugged. "'Devil's Cemetery' or something like that, if I'm not mistaken."

"A close enough translation, *cher*," the bokor said. "It had been, at one time, a graveyard for a select few, dat da

Catholic church deemed unsuited for consecrated ground. Pirates, bokor and at least one excommunicated priest had rested here, until about a hundred and twenty years ago. A hurricane swept through—da wrath of da Almighty, some said—and washed da graves out to sea. Da l'wa Ghede had protected dis place, and guarded dose who sleep wit'in from harm by da living, since time immemorial. After da loss of deir charges, da Ghede had nothing to guard...nothing to protect...and it nearly ended dem.

"Sixteen years later, a dashing white captain with a crew of...well, a very strange crew indeed...landed on da island after a valiant battle. Some of his crew were severely wounded. A few were even dead, oddly to da captain's surprise. Da captain himself suffered from a fate far worse dan any other. He was, it seemed, weary. Of da world. Of life itself. He made a deal with da Ghede, and da mambo bokor at da time, who served dem. And he and his dead shipmates have rested here, ever since." She pointed forward, past two withered weeping willows with roots jutting up from the rain-soaked soil. "Beyond da Willow Gate, lies da boneyard. Da one you seek lies wit'in, but so does da *Brave Ghede*...da Guardian of da Dead."

Greer stepped forward with an irritated sneer. "Spare us the theatrics, woman. The loa are nothing more than a demonic lie. Christian men have nothing to fear from such things." He gestured for the crew to follow him, and he moved toward the willows.

"Stop!" the bokor said. "Only three may approach da Brave Ghede and hope to appeal to his mercies. To dishonor dis command will bring death on all who enter."

Greer barked out a berating laugh, and motioned once more for his men to follow. But Finkle was the one to stop the parade of men this time. "I will remind you,

Mr. Greer, that I am in command of this expedition. I have put up with your abusive and intolerant behavior up to this point, but no more. You will respect this lady's wishes. You and I will enter, along with another of your choosing."

"But I must protest..."

"And *I* must insist. Or would you rather I choose another from your men to accompany me? I'm sure Captain Reardon would be interested to learn how you've second-guessed me at every turn."

Greer glared at the old man, then sighed. Although it was the quartermaster's job to hold the captain accountable in times when his decisions came into question—to protect the interest of the crew—he was only permitted to do so when not on the 'hunt.' Greer had harbored his doubts about Washington's quest from the very beginning—and certainly questioned Josiah Reardon's judgment in allowing this annoying old man to run command of his men—but now was definitely not the time to voice those doubts. "Very well."

He turned to his men, and appraised each one. He already knew who he'd choose, though he wanted to make a bit of a show about it. Greer was convinced that they were walking into an elaborate trap, orchestrated by brigands or pirates. The woman obviously was part of some criminal enterprise, whose job was to lure them into an ambush. The theory explained so much, including the piece of fruit thrown at him earlier. It was all part of building the expedition's apprehension, and the fool Finkle was falling for it.

So with that in mind, Greer had decided on the best possible choice to deter would-be thieves. The black man who'd been spouting the superstitious nonsense earlier. Though he was certain the man would quake in his boots from tales of evil spirits and the damned, buried within the graveyard, the slave's immense size and foreboding countenance would intimidate any would-be cutthroats lying in wait for them on the other side of the willows. Yes, he would play along with the harlot's games...for now. But he would most definitely be prepared.

"William!" he shouted, rather amused when the black man let out an involuntary squeal of apprehension. It served the oaf right for sowing the seeds of fancy among his men. "Come along, boy. Come along."

Slowly, on massive, quivering legs, the black man stepped out from the cluster of sailors around him and walked over to Greer, Finkle and the woman. "Aye, sir." His voice seemed to tremble in rhythm with his legs, eliciting a cruel smile from his quartermaster.

"I told you that you would be punished," Greer whispered, before turning to Finkle. "Are you ready?"

The old scientist nodded, and in unison they stepped toward the two ancient willows only to stop when they realized the bokor was walking in step with them.

"Where do you think you are going, witch?" Greer asked.

Gracing the officer with her most haunting smile, she pointed toward the graveyard. "Wit' you."

"Oh, I don't think so. My men, Nichols and Spratt will continue watching you while..."

"You don' be seemin' to understand your circumstances," she said. "Dis ain't no negotiation. Enter dat place wit'out me, and every one of you will be swept up to da un'erworld in seconds. Da gates of da boneyard be locked, and I'm da key."

Greer glanced over at Finkle, who shrugged. "Makes sense. She does seem to be the caretaker here. I suggest taking her seriously."

"More likely, she's simply a brigand's harlot." The quartermaster withdrew his sword, and brushed past her as he ducked under the hanging limbs of the weeping willow. "But I'll gladly acquiesce, if only to shut the two of you up."

With her customary tinkling of laughter, the woman strode forward, passing under the drooping canopy and moving ahead of the three others.

Once on the other side of the arboreal gateway, the late afternoon seemed instantly to shift to the dead of night. Where the orange-red glow of the setting sun had cut through the dense foliage like rapiers outside the graveyard, now there was nothing but darkness. If not for the warm glow of firelight from a handful of torches staked into the damp soil around them, Greer was certain they wouldn't have been able to see their hands in front of their faces.

William, towering behind him, let out a soft gasp. Greer turned to see the large man nervously giving the sign of the cross and then spitting on the ground beside his mud-caked boots.

"*Mon dieu*," the man hissed, and for once, Greer could understand the simpleton's trepidation.

"I highly doubt," Greer said, "that God has anything to do with this."

They were looking out over a circular clearing in the jungle, roughly two hundred yards in diameter. Dozens of enormous bones, sharpened at the tips, jutted up from the moist soil like the fangs of some monstrous burrowing creature digging its way up. The bones seemed to mark at least twelve distinct graves in a semi-circle around the northeast edge of the clearing. To Greer, a few of the bones appeared to be the shape of human phalanges, only the size of a tall man's femur. In the center of the graveyard, completely surrounded by jagged-tipped yellowing bones, sat a sarcophagus made entirely of sea shell fragments.

A relief carving was cut into its lid depicting a macabre visage of a gigantic skull with a hole bored into its forehead. The entire casket was covered in a strange script, painted in what looked like dried blood.

"When dey—Lanme Wa and his crew—came here a century ago, dey had been attacked," the bokor said to no one in particular. She casually strode over to the sarcophagus and brushed the tips of her finger intimately over its lid. "Attacked by creatures not seen in our world for thousands of years. Giants. Monsters wit' a thirst for blood. Most of da Cap'n's crew survived, but dese twelve didn't. Lanme Wa brought dem to dis island to be laid to rest. Dis island be a sacred place reserved for dose what da church would deem unholy. As added contempt for da giants dat had done so much harm to da crew Lanme Wa had such deep affection for, da Cap'n used deir bones to mark da graves of men he knew history would never remember. Da forgotten few what had saved da world."

There was a hissing growl from somewhere to their left, and each man turned to peer into the shadows beyond the torchlight. They paused, trying to identify the wild creature that had made the savage sound. After several moments, Greer caught the subtlest trace of movement. Three figures huddled in the shadows, dressed in what appeared to be tattered robes. The three robed creatures hissed at them, as tiny ember-red eyes burned underneath large hoods. Trembling, Greer reached for his cutlass, but the monstrous trio quickly melted once more into the jungle, before he could withdraw it.

"What in St. Peter's beard was that?" the Quartermaster asked, turning to face the bokor.

She shrugged. "Only dose wanting to pay deir respects. Dere's not'ing to fear from dem...unless you disturb dis holy ground."

"So they'll leave us alone?" Finkle asked.

When the witch nodded an affirmative, Finkle sighed and stepped toward the central sarcophagus, only to be stopped by the bokor's extended hand. "Not just yet, *cher*. Remember da Brave Ghede. He not like dose creatures, and he won't be takin' lightly to da intrusion of da livin'. Least not wit'out da proper tribute anyway."

Warily, Finkle stepped back. "You said Lanme Wa buried twelve men here. But there are thirteen graves," he said. "The sarcophagus. Is that the Captain's?"

She nodded, smiling. "It be he."

"But I don't understand. Legends suggest Lanme Wa was immortal. That he couldn't be killed. It's why we came here...to ask for his help."

"And I told you all this was mad from the beginning, Mr. Finkle," Greer spat. "We lost two good men on this unholy expedition. Men we'll need against the British. Had I known you were searching for an 'immortal' pirate, I would have called to vote Captain Reardon out of his post immediately. I'm not sure in which lunatic asylum Washington found you, but he'd do well to send you back there." Frustrated, the quartermaster kicked at the dirt under his feet, spun around to rejoin his men back in the jungle and screamed, as he stared into the jet black eyes of a giant, hissing python.

"Gentlemen," the mambo bokor declared, twirling around the central sarcophagus with melodic giggles. "Let me introduce you to da Brave Ghede."

3

The three men leapt back, their gawking eyes fixed on the enormous reptile coiled around the branch of a nearby mangrove tree. The creature's length was difficult to determine, but its width was easily three feet in diameter, and its head was the size of a small carronade.

The snake hissed at the intruders, then bobbed its head back and forth as it eyed each of them hungrily. Panicked and unable to flee the clearing through the Willow Gate, Greer spun and ran to his right, only to be stopped by a second cannon-sized snake head, just five yards away. He then turned to run in another direction, but saw that a third head bobbed and weaved, blocking that path as well.

"What devilry is this?" Greer shouted, backing away to return to the company of Finkle and William. His eyes had traced the long, sinewy necks of each snake to the centrally coiled body wrapped around the mangrove limb. *Is this three distinct creatures, or one with three heads?*

"I already tell you." The mambo bokor twirled around the sarcophagus, her arms spread wide. "Dis be da Brave

Ghede. He guards da dead from da living, and brings dose wit'out tribute to da place of da dead."

"Tribute." Finkle had his pistol calmly trained on one of the heads. "You mentioned tribute before. What kind of tribute does it require?"

She moved toward them, seeming to glide across the damp earth, as if hovering on a cushion of air. "You wish to remove Lanme Wa from dis place...wish to wake *He Who Sleeps Like Death* from his rest." Her mocha-colored fingers playfully stroked at the scruff of Finkle's chin. "If you take him, one of you must stay. One of you must be tribute to da Brave Ghede."

"Sacrifice! You're talking about human sacrifice," Finkle said.

The creature uncoiled itself from the branch, and lowered to the ground. It was indeed one monstrous snake, with three heads split unevenly along three squirming necks. The snake slithered toward them, the length of its tail still concealed by the thick jungle foliage. Each of the three heads locked on a different intruder and captured them with its gaze.

"Three heads," Finkle said. "That's why you demanded that three of us enter." He turned toward the Willow Gate, only to discover it was no longer there. It was as if the jungle itself had swallowed up the willow trees, the moment the snake had appeared.

"Three heads. One of three tributes," she said, her face was now solemn. Almost sad. "You came for Lanme Wa, but one of you must take his place."

"But he's no good to us dead!" Greer shouted, his face dripping with sweat. Shaking, he withdrew his sword, but he kept his back against William's as he watched the monstrous reptile. "We won't take him. Just let us leave this place."

"It be too late for dat now, *mon cher*. You've entered da boneyard. One of you must stay."

Greer wheeled around, pointing his cutlass at William. "Then, I choose him! Take him."

William turned, his eyes widening, and he screamed. "No! No! I serve da l'wa, too." He turned to face the serpent's central head, and bent himself into a placating bow. "I serve da l'wa, too. Please!"

Finkle leapt between the large black man and the quartermaster, slapping the flat of Greer's sword away with his hand. "Stop that, Mr. Greer. Act like a man for a change."

Greer swept his sword up to the scientist's neck. "What about him?" His wild eyes pleaded with the snakes. "He's old. He's lived his life already. Take him!"

Annoyed, Finkle turned the barrel of his gun at the quartermaster. "Mr. Greer, I will ask you again to stand down. There is no need to panic. I'm sure we can work out an amicable, mutually beneficial, treaty with this... this *jungle spirit*."

But Greer did not back down. Nor did he remove his blade from Finkle's neck, and the trio stood there in silence, staring at one another with coiled, anxious muscles. It was only at the sound of ominous hissing that they broke their gaze from one another, and turned their attention to the three-headed python. All three heads had spread apart and were now glaring at their potential targets, as streams of what looked like venomous saliva oozed from their lipless mouths.

William closed his eyes, making the sign of the cross a second time. He mouthed a silent prayer while gripping a set of pearl rosary beads from around his neck. The snakehead nearest him jerked around his shoulder, its tongue flicking closer to the man's clenched eyelids.

"Stop this, witch!" Finkle shouted. He didn't pull his eyes away from his own serpent head, but swiveled his pistol in the direction in which he guessed the mambo bokor was standing. "Call them off. Now."

"Oh, *cher*!" She whispered in his ear on the opposite side from where he thought she'd been. "If only I could. But I serve da Brave Ghede, not da other way around."

"But Greer is correct. If Lanme Wa is dead, he really is no use to us."

Still whispering in his ear, her soft lips brushed against his flesh, sending goose pimples down his neck. "I never did say he was dead, *monsieur*. I only said he was sleeping...*like* death. Dere's a difference, no?"

Slowly, Finkle turned to look at her.

She was smiling devilishly at the man, reminding Greer of a wolf before it feasted on a fallen elk. He couldn't believe what he was hearing. The crazed old man was actually believing her. He could see it in Finkle's eyes. "You're not actually considering what this...this harpy is saying, are you? Just shoot the snake, and let's be done with it!"

"Dat would not be such a good idea, I think." Suddenly, the witch was at Greer's ear, yet he'd never seen her leave Finkle's side. When she spoke to him, it had none of the playful seductiveness she'd used on the older man. "Da Brave Ghede is only now sizin' da three of you up— deciding on who it wants as tribute. Dough he look solid enough, he's made of spirit flesh. Guns won't be harmin' him none, I assure you. Nor will dat sword o' yours. So if I was you, I'd be behavin' more respectful-like, lest he decide to choose you."

The threat had its desired effect, and Greer bit down on his lips to restrain himself from speaking anymore. Though he wasn't yet ready to admit that the creature that now surrounded them was of the supernatural realm, there was no denying its ominous menace, or the three salivating heads.

Suddenly, the woman was at the black man's side, standing on bare tip-toes, and whispering into his ear as well. Greer strained to hear what she was saying, but he couldn't detect anything but the cold, harsh hiss of the python bobbing near his ear. The slave, whose eyes were still clenched tight, seemed to relax a bit when she pulled away and cast a coy smile at Greer from over William's shoulder.

"So tell us, madam," Finkle said, breaking the uncomfortable silence. "How does the selection work? What must we do to proceed? Are we expected to just stand here and wait for our doom?"

She glanced over at the central snake head, then back at the old scientist. "Da Brave Ghede says you may proceed to Lanme Wa's grave, and prepare him for his journey back to da sea. By da time you be finished, he will have chosen his tribute."

"And if we don't?" Greer's eyes widened in a silent scream when he realized the question had come from his own treacherous lips. "If we choose to leave him to rest, and return to our ship without him?"

The mambo bokor cocked her head to one side. Her glare was cold, and unsympathetic. "I thought we already spoke of dis. A tribute will be had, one way or another." She padded over to the shell sarcophagus, and beckoned them over with a hand. "Lanme Wa has slept long enough. It time he be waking up, and joining da world of da living once more. No more sulking at da cruelties he's endured. No more hiding from his destiny. Da Sea King must rise."

4

The three men moved cautiously toward the blood-covered casket in the center of the boneyard. For the first time since entering the clearing, Finkle had a chance to truly appreciate the size of the bone markers surrounding the sarcophagus. Brushing past what appeared to be a human tibia that rose up to the old man's chest, he paused a second to examine it. The bone was not calcified, but was bleached near-white by the sun. Finkle could see no fractures, artifacts or identifying marks of any kind. He turned his attention to the other bones throughout the clearing, all in perfect proportion to the one he now stood next to, and he wondered, not for the last time, from what manner of creature such bones might come. They must have indeed been some sort of giant race. The thought sent a chill down his spine, despite the fetid, stifling air of the jungle surrounding them.

"Finkle," Greer hissed, snapping him from his reverie. "Finkle, for God's sake, man...focus!"

Annoyed by the interruption, Finkle turned to face Captain Reardon's whining second-in-command. The privateer captain and he were certainly going to have a word or two about his man's behavior during this expedition. He simply would not put up with...

Finkle's train of thought came to an abrupt stop when he noticed something utterly unnerving about the strange serpentine loa that continued to vex them. The creature's trio of heads had followed them to the center of the boneyard, clearly one hundred yards from the tree line, and still its tail disappeared into the shadows of vegetation beyond. It was as if there was no end to its length, and the old man wondered if the snake was truly a creature of the supernatural, as the vodou witch doctor suggested. But before he could voice his observations, the bokor spoke once more.

"Now, messieurs," she said, her pure white smile nearly glowing in the dim torchlight. "Remove da lid, and da ritual will begin."

The three men looked to each other, then to her, then to the serpent heads and back to her again. They then eyed the monstrous skull carving on the sarcophagus's lid, and sighed resignedly.

"Fine," Finkle said. "Let's get to it, men."

"But the moment we do, that beast will take one of us," Greer said. His eyes were as wide as cannon shot. "The only thing keeping us alive is that the grave hasn't been desecrated."

"You forget, sir, we don' have much of a choice," William countered. Oddly, Finkle thought the black man's count-enance had calmed remarkably well since the bokor had whispered in his ear. He moved with a greater confidence than he had upon entering the clearing, and now, as the man spoke, he did so with a more commanding presence. His voice was deep, and rumbled as thunder with every syllable. If they managed to escape all this, Finkle felt William was a man he would very much like to get to know—to find out what the witch doctor had told him, if nothing else. "The l'wa be takin' one of us regardless. He'll take da one most deserving of tribute. Even now, he be sizing up each of our hearts. Might as well get on with what we came here to do, I say."

"Spoken like a true slave," Greer spat. But he stepped toward the sarcophagus, and took hold of one edge of the lid. Nodding to one another, Greer and Finkle grabbed hold of two corners, while William strained against both southernmost edges. "One. Two. Three!"

In unison, they heaved at the lid and nearly leapt aside as a hiss of air whistled from the opened seal. Recovering quickly, they continued to inch the lid back and forth until it slid past the casket's edge and fell to the ground with a crash.

The snake lunged toward the sarcophagus, wrapping its muscled body around the length of it three times, before bringing its heads up to stare at its potential tributes again. Finkle and Greer leapt back, but William remained fixed in his position, a wry smile spreading across his face.

What on Earth did the witch tell him? Finkle wondered. *He's so blasted confident. As if he knows he won't be chosen.*

But the loa made no move toward any of them. Instead, it simply continued hissing and watching each of the three men with eager eyes...as did the mambo bokor.

"I need blood to start da ritual. A tiny drop will do." She gestured, imitating the act of running a blade across her hand, and letting the invisible blood drip into the casket. "Don't worry now. Won't be hurtin' much 'tall."

Finkle looked to Greer, but the quartermaster shook his head adamantly. With a sigh, the scientist drew a knife from his belt, stepped to the casket and peered inside. He nearly retched at the sight. The body within had once been a rather tall man—six foot, at least—and broad in shoulder, if his decaying waistcoat and shirt were any indication. But the ravages of time had not been kind to the pirate. There was very little muscle or tissue left to support the jet black, leathery parchment of his desiccated flesh. His head was in no better shape. Although he still boasted a thick, but horribly tangled mane of dark, flowing hair, and a full, matted beard, his face was drawn, almost skeletal. His lips were so shriveled, it gave the impression of the ghastly, death's-head grin of the old Jolly Roger of bygone years. A sword, short and stubby, and unlike anything Finkle had ever seen before, rested on the pirate's chest. Finkle peered closer, and saw the strange engraving of Greek letters along the blade. The metal was too tarnished to make out what the inscription said.

It didn't matter. None of it mattered now. From looking at the shriveled body before him, he knew with disparaging certainty that they'd made this trip in vain, and that one of them would pay the ultimate price for his hubris.

"Let it be me," he whispered, slowly backing away.

"*Pardón?*"

"It's my fault. I led these men here...to this fool's errand. They shouldn't suffer for my mistake. Let the loa take me, and let them be."

The bokor cocked her head at him, as if not understanding what he was saying.

"I really must insist." His voice was louder than he'd expected, fueled by disappointment, if not a little bitterness.

"But *mon cher*, da blood hasn't been supplied yet."

"What good will that do? Lanme Wa is dead! The legends were erroneous."

"And what's it matter to you? It not your blood I be needin'." She nodded over at William, who instantly pulled his knife from its sheath, sliced at the palm of his hand and dribbled a fresh puddle of blood into the dead pirate's coffin. The moment he pulled his hand away, the serpent struck. Coiling itself around the black man's torso, it squeezed the air from his lungs before he could even scream.

"Stop!" Finkle cried, leveling his pistol at the python, and firing. The slug tore through the creature's body and impacted against a nearby tree, but the serpent continued to squeeze the life from its prize, completely unfazed. The old man turned to the bokor, his eyes pleading with her. "There's no need to kill him. Please."

She ignored him, and instead she moved over to the casket, withdrew a small glass bottle from somewhere under her dress and used it to scoop the spilled blood before corking it closed. The moment the blood was securely inside the bottle, the Brave Ghede streaked into the jungle, dragging poor William with it, before disappearing completely from sight.

"Da tribute is accepted," the bokor said.

Greer dropped to his knees, tears streaming down his face, as he repeatedly thanked the 'Lord Above' for delivering him from such a gruesome fate. Finkle, disgusted with the display, whirled around to face the bokor.

"You. Witch." His teeth were grinding together as he struggled to contain the rage building inside him.

"*Oui?*" That infernal, ever-present smile seemed to radiate out from her.

"You gave him hope, then took it away. You lied to him. He thought he was safe, and you betrayed that trust."

She nodded at this, then lifted the crimson-dripping bottle up to him. "But *mon cher*, *dis* is his hope. Dis is his promise. With dis, young William will be discovering power he never before imagined. And, after our journey's end, he'll be livin' once again...and far longer dan any o' us have ever dreamed."

5

Reardon's Mark
Off-Shore of Kavo Zile

"Absolutely not!" Captain Josiah Reardon said, slamming his fist down on his charting table. His Irish accent was so thick, it had always been difficult for Finkle to grasp every word. "I'll not have that whore of a witch anywhere near me ship."

"But Captain..."

"I'll no' have it, I tell ye. 'Tis hard enough convincin' me men to sail in these Caribbean waters, what with all these voodoo goin's on around here. But ta actually bring a mambo bokor aboard me ship? I'll have a mutiny on me hands 'fore dawn."

Finkle stared at the young captain, barely thirty years old, and already showing the ravages of 'too long in this world.' There were prematurely graying hairs speckling the corners of Reardon's temples. The crow's feet deeply cut into the corners of his eyes revealed a predisposition to laughter, but the heavy lines across his brow showed an equal amount of worry. And why shouldn't there be? The young man had already lived more in his short life than most men Finkle's age. A smuggler from Dublin, he'd been in and out of trouble with British authorities for years before receiving his letters of marque from the French. It was through the French that Finkle had first learned of the upstart Irish captain, and it was through the scientist's French connections that introductions were made. Reardon had agreed—with a few conditions—to allow his vessel to be used for their expedition.

Of course, the captain had held his own reasons for agreeing to help. With lofty ambitions, he had his eyes set on obtaining letters of marque from the Continental Navy and to earn a princely booty for wreaking havoc against the Royal merchant fleet that had sullied his name, while he served in the official navy. There was no better way to prove himself than by leading his ragtag crew of men—both patriot and cutthroat—as well as Finkle's own group, to the dangerous jungles of the Caribbean and Florida for their prize.

"And it's not just the witch, sir," the captain continued. Finkle decided to let the man vent before presenting his own side. "You cost me a good man in poor William. He'd been with me for the last three years, and was loyal as they come. And on top of it all, ye bring a disease-ridden corpse into the hold of me ship! What were ye thinkin', man?"

"I told him as such, Captain," Greer, who'd been sulking in the corner of the captain's cabin since they'd arrived, finally spoke up. "But he was much more interested in criticizing and berating me in front of the men than listening."

Reardon glared at his quartermaster in silence for a few moments, and Finkle knew he was trying to decide how to respond to that. He and Greer had served together only a short time. They'd apparently never been friends, but Greer was a trusted crewman. The captain, however, had never wanted Greer as his quartermaster on this expedition. He'd had his own man for the job, but the French outfitter, Jean Francois Torris, who'd supplied the *Mark* with its sixteen eight-pounder guns, had insisted on Greer, to pay off a debt. Greer had never let Reardon forget that he was the captain's second choice, and he had been a thorn in the captain's side the entire trip from France to the Caribbean. The quartermaster, therefore, was one thing on which both Reardon and Finkle could agree.

"Captain, if I may," Finkle said, setting his tankard down on the table and leaning back in his seat. "First of all, you have my sincerest of apologies for the loss of young William. From what I saw of him, he was a good man, and will certainly be missed. I'd offer to replace him, however, as you know, I've become a bit of an abolitionist in recent years. Freed the few slaves in my possession, and would find it distasteful to purchase another for you. However, I will be glad to make reparations for your loss in other ways."

Captain Reardon waved the issue away, then nodded for him to continue.

"Secondly, the...witch, as you call her, and the corpse are inextricably linked. One will do us no bit of good without the other."

"What good does a corpse do for us anyway? That's what I'd like to know!" Greer was now standing, pointing a long, double-jointed finger at Finkle's face.

"Greer! Sit down!" Reardon barked. The quarter-master immediately complied, and the captain returned his gaze to the older man. "He does, however, make an excellent point."

"He does. But what he doesn't realize is that I believe that the man resting in your hold below is not, in fact, dead."

"What? He is as desiccated as an Egyptian mummy, sir." Greer was back on his feet, a look of incredulity across his face. "You would have us believe he is just taking a wee nap then?"

"I had a chance to speak privately with the witch doctor as we made the trek back to shore last night," Finkle said, keeping his eyes fixed on the captain. "And while gaining a straight answer from her is no easy task, I managed to glean some tidbits of truth from her honey-dipped tongue. Lanme Wa is supposedly not dead, but is indeed, only sleeping. Now hold on. I know the very notion sounds mad, but from the stories I've read of the man, it's not beyond the impossible. After all, if you believe at all in the prize we seek, you can't believe this impossible either."

"But from Greer's account, the man has succumbed to putrefaction." Captain Reardon paced back and forth behind the chart table. "I could buy this immortality business if he just appeared to be sleeping."

"Which is exactly why we need the woman. It was her grandmother who entombed him—at his own request—and it is the younger witch who knows how to revive him. But it will take time. More time than we have to waste upon this island." Finkle shrugged. "What harm could come from letting her remain aboard until our next port? If she's not revived him, we'll set both of them off the ship, and will be on our way to Florida."

Reardon continued to pace, considering the old man's argument. He then stopped, and glanced out the bay windows of his aft-side cabin, looking out at the silver reflection of moonlight off the white-crested surf outside. They were still anchored, just two hundred yards off shore of the island, and the waves were slowly building, rocking the twin-masted cutter back and forth in rhythmic chops.

The captain rubbed at his scruff-covered chin, obviously in turmoil as to the next phase of the plan. Then, slowly, he turned around to face Finkle, his head shaking.

"I'm sorry," he said. "I just can't see where the benefits outweigh the risk. That woman is trouble, with the blackest of hearts. I kin see it in her green eyes. If we let her remain on board, there'll be hell to pay for it. I can promise ye that."

"But I really must insis..."

A sudden commotion from above—the sound of thirty-six pairs of feet running to and fro on the deck above—broke out, cutting Finkle's protestations off in mid-sentence. Two seconds later, there was a pounding on the captain's door.

"Cap'n! Cap'n! Sails! We've got sails on the horizon, and they're flyin' pirate colors!"

Captain Reardon bolted for the door, and swung it open. He ran up the stairs, onto the upper deck, with Greer and Finkle following close behind. Once on deck, they met the Irish captain at the foot of the bowsprit where he already had a glass up to his right eye.

"Well, I'll be..." Reardon handed the glass to Finkle, who brought it to his own eye to take in the large, square-rigged man-o-war sailing straight for them. "I ain't heard of colors like that bein' used in nearly a hundred years."

Finkle knew precisely what the captain meant as he stared, slack-jawed, at the waving black flag with a white skeleton wearing a golden crown atop its head. Except for the crown, it was the traditional flag of the pirates of old—the kind of pirates that hadn't been seen in these waters since the days of Calico Jack and Blackbeard. But it was the crown that sent a gut-wrenching chill down Finkle's spine.

"The *Presley's Hound*," he whispered.

"What?"

"Lanme Wa's ship. It was the name of his ship. Legends say his crew lay in wait to protect him from any who might seek him out," Finkle said. His mouth was suddenly dry, and he felt a disturbing desire for rum as he continued to stare out at the ship that surely must have come from hell itself. "When we encountered no resistance on the island, I'd just assumed the warnings were the stuff of myth. Or that the crew had long ago died away. I never imagined we'd encounter them at sea."

A sudden image flashed through the scientist's mind. The strangely cloaked figures in the boneyard. Their hisses still chilled him to the bone. And he wondered if Lanme Wa's accursed crew had been on the island after all.

"Captain." A sailor—Spratt, Finkle believed was his name—ran up to Reardon out of breath. "That's a frigate. There's no way we can take 'em harbored as we are in this lagoon."

Reardon turned to Finkle. "Would they fire on us? If they're really Lanme Wa's crew, and they're protecting their captain, would they dare fire upon the ship that has him in its hold?"

The scientist nodded grimly. "He's supposed to be immortal. To them, it's better to sink the ship, then later dive down to retrieve him. I don't think they'd have a bit of concern firing on us, no."

Reardon looked out across the western horizon, then turned to Greer. "Ready the main sails."

"Sir? What about the corpse and the witch?" Greer asked.

"Mr. Greer, we ha' six eighteen-pound cannons, and ten swivel guns. That man-o-war has at least thirty-six cannons at her disposal. Need I repeat meself?"

Greer shook his head.

"Good, then raise anchor, and let's outrun these brigands before they get within range."

When the quartermaster stalked away, barking orders to the crew, Captain Reardon turned to Finkle, and sighed. "I reckon, Mr. Finkle, you need to introduce me to this bokor of yours. We may need her juju 'fore journey's end."

6

Finkle led the captain down below deck, and into the crew's quarters, where a series of hanging sheets closed off the bokor's sleeping chamber from the rest of the crew. Cautiously, Finkle tapped on a wooden beam supporting one of the sheets.

"*Oui?*" came the soft voice of the mambo bokor.

"It's Jim Brannan Finkle, madam. Along with Captain Reardon," Finkle said. "We were hoping for a moment of your time."

The ship shifted as it caught its headwind, came around and began tacking in a northwest direction. The scientist grabbed hold of the beam, readying himself for the sound of pursuing cannon fire, but it didn't come. A moment later, the sheet was pulled back to reveal the beautiful Creole woman, now completely nude. Only her smile distracted Finkle's eyes away from her sleek, taut frame.

"It is my pleasure to make your acquaintance, Captain." She held out her hand, palm down, in the fashion of a lady expecting a kiss.

Reardon blushed, then seemed to gather his wits. "For cryin' out loud, put some clothes on, lass! If me crew were to see you this way, I'm not sure I could guarantee yer safety."

Still smiling, she glanced down at her sweating skin, spread her arms out in a freeing gesture and sighed. "But *mon Capitaine*, it is necessary for da magicks I must do to raise up Lanme Wa. On land, I go barefoot, to draw closer to da earth. But on da sea...da sea is much more powerful than da land. Da sea elevates da l'was' might a great deal... especially with the blood magick necessary for our needs. Even so, dere should be as few barriers between me and da sea as possible. Clothing only hinders da ritual."

"Well, at least for now, please cover yourself with a sheet or something," Finkle said, grabbing a sheer linen sheet resting on a nearby crate, and handing it to her. "We need to go visit our pirate friend at once, and the crew cannot see you in such a state of undress."

With a slight shrug, she accepted the sheet, and wrapped herself in it, but she kept her shoulders to her collarbone bare. She then grabbed a leather bag, decorated with an assortment of bones and sea shells, stepped out from her makeshift bedchamber and nodded. "All right. So take me to Lanme Wa, and let's get started."

The trio slipped through the two rows of hammocks and bunks cluttering the sleeping quarters below deck. The ship seemed to be making good speed now, and they were forced, on more than one occasion, to grab hold of the nearest beam, rope or handle they could find, to keep from toppling over as they crashed through the waves. Ninety-three feet aft, they came to the hold, and Reardon unlocked the door with his key, before swinging it open and gesturing for them to enter. Once inside, he lit a candle on a table next to the door, and lifted it to light the room.

The entire space had been emptied, save for the wooden crate Reardon's men had used to transport the mummified remains to the ship. The three walked over to it, and the captain handed Finkle the candle, then reached down to retrieve a crowbar leaning against the wall.

"Can I open it?" Reardon asked the bokor.

She nodded her assent, and he set to work loosening the nails that held the crate's lid. A few minutes later, the lid was pulled aside and Reardon stared open-mouthed down into the box.

"By all that's holy..." He glanced to Finkle, then to the woman. "You expect me to believe you can bring this...this *thing* back to life? You must think me daft!"

She looked up at him, with amused, gleaming eyes. "I never said I could bring ol' Lanme Wa back from da dead."

"What?" Finkle wheeled around to gape at her. "But you said..."

"I said he be only sleepin', *mon cher*. He ain't dead. Never has been, so far as I know." She reached down into the crate, and brushed a long, stray hair from out of the body's eyes. The gesture was tender. Almost loving. "No, he's not dead a'tall. We merely need to coax him awake, and he'll be as good as new in no time."

Reardon glanced over at Finkle, a single eyebrow raised. "Ye told us the pirate is supposed to be immortal."

Finkle nodded. "That's what the legends say."

"And that he was so feared that Blackbeard hisself turned tail and ran at the sight of his colors."

"That's true." Finkle glanced down at the leathery figure laying prone in the crate. "What are you getting at, Captain?"

Reardon turned his attention back to the mambo bokor. "Well, I'm curious. If this man was truly as you say, what on Earth would compel him to climb into a sarcophagus and...and turn into that?" He pointed down at the body.

The bokor continued to stroke at Lanme Wa's tangled beard. "Because he done lived too long. Was beginnin' to lose himself. Beginning to forget da world he come from, and forget da kind of man he was, before all this happened to him." She lovingly began straightening the corpse's fraying cravat, then continued. "He lost too many friends. Lost too many battles not fought with powder or steel, but with da heart. He begun to grow cold. Indifferent to da world, and dere were only two things keepin' him grounded to his old life...a woman and a daughter. But dey were just too far away to reach, so he chose to rest in da grave 'til he could draw closer to dem dat he loved. Dat's why he sleepin' now. Bidin' his time."

The scientist and the captain stood in silence for several long moments, reflecting on what she had just told them. Finally, Finkle spoke up. "Are you telling us the man had gone mad? If he awakens, will he be better suited for the lunatic asylum than an expedition?"

"Oh, make no mistake, *cher*...when he wakes, he'll be none too happy. But he's as sane as any man who ever did live. Though, perhaps, sadder. And bitter. But he's an honorable man at heart, I can tell you. His wrath will be stirred, dere's no doubt...but once he settles down...once he learns about your quest, he'll calm down nice enough." Then, without further preamble, she shucked off the sheet to reveal her finely-toned nakedness, opened up her medicine bag and pointed toward the door to the hold. "Now, let me do my work in private. He'll be waking soon enough."

7

"I don't trust her," Reardon said, as the two climbed the ladder to the quarterdeck.

"Neither do I." Finkle had been growing even more uneasy about the female witch doctor with every given second. She still hadn't explained to him the strange exchange she'd had with William before his death. Even more unsettling, Finkle wasn't entirely sure why she had insisted on accompanying the crew on their expedition. She had made pitiful claims about the necessity of her presence in reviving Lanme Wa, but Finkle couldn't help but feel it had all been a ruse of some kind. If the pirate was, as she claimed, alive and in some strange form of hibernation, Finkle couldn't understand why she was needed at all. Surely there were more mundane ways to wake the pirate other than her so-called magic. "But right now, I don't believe we have much choice. For better or worse, we're stuck with her. The pirates' sudden arrival saw to that."

"Speaking of..." Reardon glanced up toward the rigging, and caught sight of the man he was looking for, nestled in the ship's crow's nest. "Needles!"

"Aye, Cap'n!" The man called Needles, the ship's lookout, shouted down.

"Any sign of our pursuers?"

"Aye! They're two miles northeast, and holdin' steady. For some reason, they've reefed their sails."

Reardon's eyes narrowed. "Why would they possibly do that?" He suddenly bolted to the stern, pulled his glass from the pouch attached to his belt and looked out to the northeast horizon. "It makes no sense."

"What? What's wrong?" Finkle asked, huffing from chasing after the captain.

"The *Mark* is one of the fastest ships around. Even armed as we are, we're sitting at just under a hundred and fifty tons." He nodded toward the *Hound*. "That frigate is easily four hundred. I've not been able to fathom how they've done it, but they've been keepin' pace with us since we left that cursed island. Hardly put any effort into it, I'd wager. But Needles is right. They've reefed their sails. They could easily catch us up, but they've intentionally slowed themselves. They're coming to a stop."

"Why would they do that?"

The captain looked up at the sky and the purple-orange haze of the approaching dawn. Then he shrugged. "No idea. That's what concerns me." He eyed the ship through the glass again, and Finkle could sense the man's muscles tensing underneath his frock coat. "No matter the reason, we need to take advantage of it and put as much distance between us and them as we can... before they change their mind."

The mambo bokor had gone by many names throughout her short thirty-one years on Earth, but the name bestowed upon her by her grandmother was Asherah. It was a family name, passed down from mother to daughter for generations, and marking each name-bearer as a future mambo bokor. Only the daughters who had the gift of vodou could be called by this name, and she had worn it well since her grandmother's death.

Now, however, she was on the verge of taking the name to levels not dreamed of since the Philistine goddess of her namesake, who the Arabs called Ishtar. The place these white men were taking her would ensure she would never want for anything again. Once more, the mention of her name would bring men to their knees, as it had in days long ago. Though the white men had been cautious with their tongues—had never verbally conveyed the object of their quest—she knew full well what they sought. Knew they had mistakenly believed Lanme Wa had already found it, and they hoped he would guide them to it.

But the pirate, though he had indeed searched for it in his travels, had never actually located it. Had, in fact, given up on it being real, and had turned his attentions to other pursuits. Asherah, however, knew better. She knew it existed, and she understood that the power to be gained from the expedition would bring nations crashing down in ruins. It would also set her up as the one true goddess of the New World.

This, of course, was why the poor slave, William, was so important. Why she'd influenced the *Brave Ghede* to take him, and not the bothersome Greer. Smiling, she reached into her medicine pouch and retrieved the vial of blood she'd scooped from Lanme Wa's casket. She then placed the vial in the center of a circle of salt she'd poured onto the floor. Next she mumbled an indecipherable prayer.

When she finished, she turned to the box in which Lanme Wa lay, and sneered. "Don't you be judgin' me, pirate. For too long, my line has been servin' you. Da service you gave my great-grandmother has long since been repaid, and now it be time we take our rightful place in dis world."

She didn't expect him to answer her challenge. She doubted he was even aware of what was going on. Asherah hadn't lied to the funny old scientist and the ship's captain, though.

Lanme Wa was most definitely alive.

Throughout the years, she'd seen the signs. From the age of six, her grandmother had charged her with the task of feeding the man once a year. The chore usually consisted of some arcane ritual she'd never fully understood. Then they would push back the sarcophagus's lid, and she would toss in a single fruit—a mango, orange or even an apple, when they were available. A month later, Asherah was supposed to return to the crypt, open it and remove whatever was left. On every single occasion, the fruit showed signs of having been eaten—if only a bite or two. And since the casket was sealed airtight, she knew the food had not been co-opted by any scavenging rats. For even if they could have gotten inside, they would have quickly died from suffocation.

No, Asherah had no doubt that the pirate known as Lanme Wa was still alive, and capable, at least, of eating. She wasn't entirely sure what else the desiccated living corpse was capable of... If he was aware of his surroundings... If he could hear the words being spoken around him. But there was one thing she knew all too well. She knew that once the immortal pirate awakened, he would pose the greatest threat to her plans, and she would need all the help she could get to overcome him.

That, of course, brought her thoughts around full circle to William. The young slave was the key. The l'wa, who she served, were territorial. Their influence and power could be felt only in the place where they were created. Once she had stepped onto the ship, and left the safety of the Caribbean islands she called home, the l'wa she knew so well were useless to her. A l'wa created in the turmoil of the raging sea, however, would have powers far beyond those of any she'd known her entire life. All she needed was a willing soul, and William had agreed enthusiastically.

She rifled through her medicine bag again, withdrew seven candles made of dolphin lard, and an assortment of herbs, shredded tobacco leaf, sugar cane stalks and a bottle of snake venom. She placed each on the floor. Satisfied all the ingredients were present, Asherah carefully set each candle around the circle of salt, then lit each of them in counterclockwise order.

Now, for the elements of life.

She sprinkled three small piles of the tobacco, representing the haze of the future, around the blood vial. Then, uncorking the snake venom, she poured the contents along the outline of the circle while reciting the necessary incantation to withdraw the veil of death. The stalks of sugar cane were arranged on the floor in the form of a cross, which was designed to give a newborn l'wa the sweet taste of wisdom and power. Finally, taking a pinch of the herbs, she dropped it into the wide-mouthed neck of the blood vial, before immediately going to each candle and blowing out the flames.

The sickly sweet aroma of the candle's smoke wafted up toward her nostrils, and she inhaled deeply before swaying back and forth to an inaudible tune playing in the back of her mind. Unconsciously, she sung the words of the ancient song, focusing her will on the vial and imagining the thick, strong frame of William in her mind's eye. Five minutes later, as the last vestiges of smoke had completely disappeared, she reached down, corked the vial of blood and smiled.

Now, all that was left was to reach their destination. She would have one of the most powerful l'was ever conjured, and it would be fully tied to American soil. It was only a matter of time, and there was nothing Lanme Wa could do to prevent it.

A sudden tap at the door startled her from her reverie. *"Oui?"*

"Sorry, ma'am," came a quivering voice from the other side of the hold's door. "The cap'n was wonderin' how much longer it'll be. Them pirates is keepin' a tight path on our stern, and he's thinkin' their cap'n might be needed come night fall."

Asherah glanced back over at the crate, and rolled her eyes. As far as she was concerned, Lanme Wa could sleep til his heart's content, but she knew Captain Reardon wasn't going to allow her that luxury. On the other hand, she honestly did not know how to revive the pirate. It was a lesson never taught her by her grandmother.

When it be time for Lanme Wa to awaken, her grandmother had always told her, *Lanme Wa will awaken. Not a minute sooner.*

Asherah pulled the sheet around her once more, strode over to the door and opened it. The young cabin boy jumped back with a yelp, causing the mambo bokor to laugh. She cherished the power she had over these white men—both from fear, as well as from lust—and she savored every reminder of the awe they had for her.

"Tell *mon Capitaine* I need eight strong hands to carry Lanme Wa to da upper deck."

With a curt salute, the boy scampered up the ladder and disappeared. Ten minutes later, four large sailors and

Quartermaster Greer returned to the hold. The Englishman, whom Asherah could sense was not well-liked among
his mostly Irish crew, directed the men to the wooden
crate without so much as glancing at her. She then
watched as the hatch above the hold was opened, and a
crane hook was lowered down. The men carefully secured
the crate, and with a series of shouted commands from
Greer, it was lifted up to the deck.

"Now, woman," Greer said with a sneer. He refused to
look her in the eye. "Please dress yourself in more *civilized*
attire, and meet the Captain and Mr. Finkle topside, as
soon as possible."

With that, he motioned to his men to follow him, and
they left her alone in the hold to reflect on her own
amusement.

8

After changing back into her linen shift, Asherah made her way up on deck to see Captain Reardon, Jim Brannan Finkle and a handful of crew standing over the opened crate. Greer was nowhere to be seen. Three sailors were vigilantly watching the sea from the bow of the ship, while their compatriots tended to various other duties.

The ship rocked hard from side-to-side, as it was bombarded by choppy waves originating from dark skies to the west. She didn't need to see the clouds beyond to know that a storm was approaching. She could taste it on the rush of wind brushing past her face, and she inhaled deeply, savoring the sweet tang of the rapidly cooling air.

Turning her attention back to the captain, she strode over to them, and greeted Reardon with a slight nod of her head. "*Capitaine* Reardon."

"The time for pleasantries is long past, lassie," he said, pointing to the crate. "Though I'm mightily vexed as to how a pirate's crew can still be sailing more than a hundred years after their captain's death...or whatever you call it. The sad fact o' the matter is, they are. Though they've intentionally slowed their pursuit since daybreak, they're still trackin' us from the southeast. On top of that, we're fast approachin' a hell of a storm to the west, and so far, you've not earned your keep aboard me ship."

"And how you think I should help, *cher*? More important, how you think Lanme Wa can help? He be immortal. Not a god. He can't turn da weather 'round to go de other way."

"But he may be able to call off his crew," Finkle said. Of all the men she'd encountered so far on this expedition, he was the one that unnerved her the most. Though he was far advanced in years, he had a spirit about him stronger than any of the younger men on the crew. And a wisdom that might just see through her ruse, if she wasn't more vigilant around him. On the other hand, he continued to show her nothing but the utmost kindness—not out of fear or desire, as with the other sailors, but from something more akin to respect. And it was this that worried her more than anything else. "This would allow us to sail around the storm, and avoid a possible catastrophe. As it stands, if our course changes even slightly, Lanme Wa's crew could overtake us in minutes, and all would be lost anyway."

She glanced back to the stern, catching a brief glimpse of square sails, just as the bow swept up over a swell, and then the pirate ship was gone from view once more. She already knew what she was going to do, but she needed to continue the charade for as long as she could. Truth was, there was no magical incantation to revive the immortal pirate. No spell, potion or ritual. Her grandmother was right. He would wake up when it was time for him to wake up, and not a minute later or sooner. The question was whether or not she could hasten his timetable, and to do what she had in mind would require a great deal of risk. If she failed, Captain Reardon and

Finkle would have no further need of her. She would surely be cast overboard for failure to live up to her end of the bargain. That would definitely put the nails to her carefully laid plans, and she would have none of it. This would simply have to work.

"Very well," she said, nodding to the crate. "Remove him, and place him on da deck."

Reardon instructed his men to do as she said, and within minutes, the mummified pirate was sprawled across the tar-covered planks. She knelt down beside him, reached into her medicine bag and withdrew a bottle of red dye she'd concocted from a variety of tropical flowers on the islands she most frequented. Opening the bottle, she dipped her index finger into the warm, sticky liquid.

"Remove his shirt."

The sailors stared at her in horror. Two of them took a step back.

"You two." Captain Reardon pointed to the two who had backed away. "Thanks for volunteerin', lads. Get to it."

Scrunching up their noses in disgust, the two sailors shuffled forward, bent down, and began the repulsive task of cutting away the pirate's linen shirt. Surprisingly, the shirt was relatively dry, and clean—save for a healthy coating of dust. It was not at all covered in the viscous bodily fluids of a corpse desiccated over time. Still, one sailor's mouth clamped shut and swelled with nausea, before he dashed over to the rail, vomiting over the side. His partner finished the task, and Asherah shooed him away before inscribing a series of symbols over Lanme Wa's upper torso with her dye-covered finger. The symbols were meaningless, of course. Simply for show. But no one on board the *Mark* would know that. When she was satisfied with her work, she looked up at the captain. "Now is da time you'll be needin' to trust me. Trust me more than you have so far."

"What? What do you need me to do?"

She looked down into Lanme Wa's pruned, cloudy eyes, closed his flaking eyelids and frowned. "You be needin' to keelhaul him."

"Keelhaul!" Finkle blurted. "Are you mad, woman? The reason you're here is to revive him—if possible. Not kill him."

"It da only way, *cher.*"

"But even if keelhauling him doesn't tear him apart, those waters are crawling with sharks."

"Aye," Reardon agreed. "Needles just saw a school of hammerheads about two miles to the south. In his condition, they'll be drawn to him like flies to molasses."

Asherah shook her head. "I'm sorry. It truly be da only way. He be needin' da salt and water of life to revive him bones. Without dat, he just a shriveled up corpse on da deck of dis ship."

"Captain, I really must protest," Greer said. The man had seemed to materialize from nowhere.

"Why am I not surprised?" Reardon said, shaking his head.

The quartermaster ignored the comment. "Keelhauling was abolished more than twenty years ago. What kind of example would we be setting..."

"The pirate's as good as dead anyway, Mr. Greer. As far as I'm concerned, that is. Keelhaulin' ain't that much of a punishment to him, now is it?"

"But..."

"Spratt! Smally! Front and center!" The captain shouted. Two sailors rushed up, and stood at attention. "Let's get this man ready for a keelhaul, gentlemen. If nothin' else, we'll at least be feedin' the local fish."

The two sailors procured a long coil of rope, and began barking orders at their fellow crewmen. Asherah watched as they tied Lanme Wa to the center of the line, while another group of sailors dragged the other end of the rope over the bow, then brought it to the center of the ship.

"Be sure to give it some slack, gents." Captain Reardon bent down to help his men pick up the corpse, and carry it to the port side rail. "Don't want his leathery hide gettin' scored by the razor-sharp edges of barnacles down below, now do we?"

Reardon, gripping the pirate's right arm, looked over at Asherah.

"Give him a dagger," she said. "Tuck it in his belt."

He cocked his head at her.

"Dis won't be no typical keelhaul, *mon cher*. Once you get him directly under da ship, you'll be needin' to leave him dere for a bit."

"For how long?" Finkle asked, dabbing a handkerchief against his perspiring forehead.

"Til he uses dat knife to cut away da rope, and climb back on board."

Each man on deck stopped what they were doing, and stared at her. She couldn't resist the urge to smile at their obvious discomfort. For the first time since finding Lanme Wa, the sheer gravity of what they were attempting to do had finally hit home. They were, in fact, attempting to resurrect the decomposed corpse of a long dead pirate. And if this worked, that same pirate would be scrambling back on board their very ship. If Asherah was honest with herself, she would have to admit that the thought sent a twinge of fear down her spine, as well.

"And if he doesn't?" Reardon broke the silence in a low, conspiratorial voice.

"Den dis has all been in vain, no?"

The captain glared at her for a split second, then nodded at his men. The corpse was thrown over the side.

There was a muffled splash, and suddenly, the rope pulled taut as Lanme Wa was dragged helplessly under the ship.

9

The darkness embraced him. Blissful oblivion wrapped its cold, apathetic arms around his emaciated frame, protecting him from the life he'd begun to despise. How long had it been this way? A day? A month? A millennium? It was impossible to say, but he welcomed it with all his heart.

His mates—his *friends*, yes, that was the correct word—would say he'd given up. But they couldn't possibly know. Couldn't possibly understand. Then again, he wasn't entirely certain if he even had any friends. Not anymore. They'd gradually started to become lost to him through time. Just as an adult has only the vaguest of recollections of childhood friends long gone, his own memories had begun to fade centuries ago. Only the faintest of recollections could bring them to mind...and then only by chance. The briefest whiff of a fragrance. A particular shade of red. A shadow of a large man standing before the sun. These triggered those fleeting memories he so longed for. But they were growing far too dim for any sustainable accuracy.

There were only two faces from his *First Life*—as he had begun thinking of it—that were ingrained deeply within his soul, though even now he struggled to recall their names in the form of English he'd not spoken in over two thousand years. The woman, he loved dearly. Had been faithful to her all this time. Had not given his heart to another—not even been tempted to do so. The girl was something else entirely. She wasn't his daughter by birth. That much he could remember. But his heart ached for her more than it would for a thousand daughters. He missed her bright, intelligent smile. That glimmer of mischief in her eyes when she'd done something she wasn't supposed to. They'd shared so much together in her short few years, but he couldn't imagine his life without her.

Only, he *had* been without her. And the woman. And it had been eating him alive for centuries. When even their faces had begun to fade, he knew it was time. Time to...

He felt a crushing weight against his chest, twisting his thoughts back to the present. Something pushed against his body. A dull throbbing, vibrating up and down every one of his nerves. Then came a burning sensation. A white-hot fire searing into his lungs. He'd experienced this sensation before—on multiple occasions. But he couldn't gather enough wits to remember what it had been.

Something... *What was the word? Liquid.* Wet. Salty. Was rushing past his lips, flooding his throat and pouring down into his...his...*lungs? Is that the right word? Yes. Lungs.*

He was submerged. Underwater.

His eyes snapped open. Something hard and flakey cracked as his lids pulled back from his cloudy eyes. The world around him was hazy. Dark. The saltwater burned at his eyes, and he blinked back the pain, trying to clear his vision. But his eyes had been useless within the sarcophagus for far too long. It would take some time to recover his vision. For now, however, he knew the important thing was to pull himself to the surface. Though he knew he wouldn't die, his brain did need oxygen to function properly. It wouldn't do him much good to survive, if he spent his immortality on the bottom of the sea, unable to rise from a watery grave.

He tried moving his arms, but they were stiff. Felt brittle, like two old pieces of lumber charred from a campfire. He pushed through it, bending his elbows and hearing the sound of atrophied muscles and tendons tearing and popping as he moved. Instantly a white, hot fire burned at the inside of his elbows, and he winced. Or at least, he made a reasonable attempt. He clamped down on his dry, cracked lips, trying to prevent himself from taking in any more water than he had already. After several long moments, his hands pulled up to his waist to find a thick hemp rope tied with a slip knot. Blindly, he grabbed at the rope and pulled. Immediately he felt the pull returned. Someone was most definitely on the other end of the line. He jerked down on the line again, and felt a second reply from the other end.

Suddenly, he jerked forward in the water as the rope pulled taut around his waist, and he began to be pulled up toward the surface. For the first time since his mind awakened from its slumber, he felt the cool water rush over his cheeks, and through his long tangled hair. It was unnerving to him just how refreshing the sensation was. How it soothed his flaking desiccated skin. He could feel the cells of his body already mending. Already healing the damage that had been done by allowing himself to drift off into undeath. It hadn't been the first time he'd tried it, but it evidently had been the longest amount of time he'd spent in the grave. The way he felt, he told himself he'd never do it again, but he wasn't sure that was the truth. It ultimately depended on how much time was left. How much longer he'd have to wait to return to...to...

He screamed a silent scream over the frustration of not remembering their names. Of all people to forget, how could he forget them? They were the reason he'd managed to go on for as long as he had, and...

Something sharp and powerful crunched down on his leg, and yanked him back toward the ocean floor. His ascent to the surface abruptly stopped, and he felt the sharp sting of his tibia splitting in two from the impact. He twisted in the water, focusing his eyes as best he could. He saw a ghastly serpentine shape thrashing through the water on the other end of his leg. The shape was long—easily larger than fifteen feet—with a sharply pointed fin jutting up from its back. A powerful, two-pronged tail whipped back and forth, as its massive hammer-shaped head wrenched at the flesh of his useless leg.

Son of a...

He let go of the rope, and his right hand brushed past something cold and metallic tucked into his belt. He reached for it, and felt the bone-carved handle of some type of dagger. Forcing the pain into the back of his mind—a trick he'd perfected over the centuries—he grabbed hold of the knife, yanked it from his belt and blindly slashed down at the massive hammerhead. The blade glanced across the shark's rough skin to little effect. But the blow startled the animal enough to ease up on his leg. It was just enough for him to jerk himself outside of the creature's immediate reach. As he did so, he watched as the unfocus-ed object that could only be his lower leg drifted away and slowly sank to the ocean's floor.

The hammerhead, sensing the limb's descent, dove headfirst toward it. Its tail wagged frantically to propel it toward its leathery meal. Fortunately, the old pirate had very little blood left within him to bleed out. He watched as only a small, six-inch cloud of dark fluid leaked from his leg wound.

Sensing this was his chance, he tugged on the rope once more with his free hand, and felt it jerk him toward the surface once more. He glanced up. Though his vision was still hindered by years of slumber, he could just make out the darkening sky above him. It appeared that clouds loomed overhead. The makings of a storm. And rocking from side to side, just a few feet to his right, was the keel-shaped shadow of a small ship—a cutter of some kind, not his own frigate.

As he ascended, propelled by reformed muscles and sinews, he peered down again just in time to see the hammerhead rushing hungrily toward him. Even worse, two others were approaching from just under the ship. The puny purge of blood that had seeped from his leg had drawn the creatures straight to him. Tethered to the rope as he was, he was little more than fish bait with no room to move around. The sharks had the advantage of the sea at their disposal, but he had millennia of experience. It was he, not these creatures, that was the apex predator here, and before this day was out, he was going to show them.

With a flick of his wrist, he cut through the rope securing him to the cutter, whipped around in the water, and immediately began swimming toward the closest shark. The grin on his face matched those of the animals he faced. Sharp and infinitely deadly.

"Cap'n!" cried one of the sailors on the other end of the line.

Reardon turned to see the man gripping the sliced end of the rope.

"Bloody 'ell." He stalked over to the man, and took the rope from him with a jerk. A brief glance revealed what happened. "He cut the blasted thing."

Finkle moved over to them, and examined it. "Now, why on Earth would he do something like that?"

Reardon shrugged. "Maybe he saw the *Hound*? Maybe he's attempting to swim his way to them?"

"I don't think so, Cap'n," another sailor, Mr. Leighfield, said. "We felt him pullin' on the line. We begun draggin' him back up, then something yanked him back down hard. Figure he was maybe bein' attacked by one of them sharks we seen earlier. Then a minute later, he tugged again. We began pullin' him back up... Then we had nothin' on the line."

Reardon whipped his head around toward the mambo bokor. "Witch! What do you think this means?"

"Got no idea, *Capitaine*," she said, cocking her head to the left, as if listening to something. "But I think your sailor dere be on to something. If dere be sharks in dose waters, and dey be after Lanme Wa for supper, den Lanme Wa is likely to fight back. Leashin' him to da ship will only hinder his power. Make sense for him to cut hisself free. It why I insisted he be given da dagger."

Reardon rolled his eyes. He was beginning to wonder if the rewards from this expedition would ever outweigh the ordeal itself.

"Mr. Winfield!" he cried.

"Aye, Cap'n!" Mr. Winfield responded from behind the wheel.

"Turn us about! We need to go back for our cargo!"

"But Captain, I have to protest." Greer jogged up to the captain, dabbing a handkerchief across his brow. "Those pirates out there will blow us from the water if we stray too close. It's foolish to go back for that...that corpse."

"Beggin' pardon, sir," Leighfield said, raising a hand humbly. "Wasn't no corpse tuggin' on the line. Wasn't snagged on anythin' either. There was intelligence behind the pull, I can tell ye that much. Whatever he is down there, he ain't dead. Least, not when he gave the tug anyway." Then, as if the concept fully dawned on the young sailor, he crossed himself, bowed his head and mumbled a quick prayer to St. Nicholas, the patron saint of sailors.

"Your misgivings have been heard and duly noted, Mr. Greer," Captain Reardon said with a sneer. "And also ignored. The *Presley's Hound*'s no' moved an inch since we submerged Lanme Wa, and there's no reason to expect 'em to attack now, while their captain is in such a harrowing position. Now return to your post, and keep an eye on that man-o-war, sir. Just in case." The quartermaster sniffed, and then returned to the port side rail to keep watch on the frigate. Reardon watched him leave, then turned back to the bokor. "You realize if he was attacked by sharks down there, there'll be little left of him to collect, lass."

She shrugged, but maintained her usual cool smile.

"And you also know what happens to you should our cargo become unusable to us?"

"What are you suggestin', *mon cher*? You brought me on to awaken him. From your own men's account, I did what I was employed to do."

"I'm suggestin' you may want to start prayin' to those heathen gods of yours. Work whatever vile magicks at your disposal to see that walkin' corpse keeps a'walkin'."

Her smile broadened. "Der's no need to fear 'bout dat. You just go back to where we lost him, and Lanme Wa will handle da rest. You just watch 'nd see."

10

The first of the sharks rolled over on its side, a jagged gash stretching underneath its jaw and gushing a crimson fount into the water. The man once known as Jack Sigler, callsign: King, the immortal leader of a twenty-first century black-ops group known as Chess Team, who was sent back and lost in time, tried yanking the dagger out of the creature's rough hide. The blade, however, snagging against cartilage, snapped in two, rendering it useless. Unperturbed, he dropped the knife handle and whirled around to face his two other attackers. His lungs throbbed. His vision, still cloudy but improving, was dotted with splotches of red and green. The oxygen in his blood was running low, and his lungs were filled with water. If he didn't do something about that now, he would pass out soon. He'd been through a great deal throughout his long life. Being eaten and digested by a large, hungry predator was not something he wanted to experience again. He wasn't certain either, how exactly he'd regenerate if his pieces were scattered between two different creatures.

Fortunately, the rush of blood flowing from their fallen comrade sent the other two hammerheads into a frenzy. They shot past him, lunging toward the dead shark drifting to the bottom. They wrenched flesh away from its bones with whipping snaps of their heads. Using the distraction, King shot toward the surface. Although his ascent was encumbered by his severed right leg, he broke through and gulped in a heaving breath. The moment the air coursed down his trachea, his body convulsed in a fit of hacking coughs. Doubling over, he began sinking again, managed to regain a modicum of control and paddled up to the surface once more.

Treading water, he cleared his mind. Focused his thoughts on slowly working his lungs and diaphragm, and eased the excess water up past his lips. Once satisfied his lungs were clear, he cautiously inhaled another deep breath, and he savored the blood-nourishing oxygen. Immediately, he felt a tingle in his lower leg. The addition of air had already set his body to mending his injuries. It was only a matter of time before his severed leg would be whole once more. He need only hold out long enough and he'd soon have the mobility needed to deal with the predators hunting him.

Relaxing, he took the briefest of seconds to collect his thoughts. They were still sluggish. Primal even. If he hoped to endure, he needed to take stock of his situation.

He glanced out over the horizon, scanning from right to left. To the southeast, the cutter was turning about in a slow sweeping arc. The crew was apparently returning for him. Further south, the dark clouds of the oncoming storm loomed. Streaks of searing white energy flashed through the angry sky, while sheets of rain pelted the sea just twenty miles away. It wouldn't be long before the ocean would become enraged, tossing him about like a broken rag doll within the tempest.

Behind him, and to the north, he caught sight of a three-masted ship with gray, square sails. A black flag flapped near the stern of the large frigate, but the crew made no attempt to come to his aid. He smiled. Of course they wouldn't. Not until the clouds had completely blocked out the sunlight, or night fell. Whichever came first.

But he was running out of time. The two sharks would soon be finished with their meal, and they would be on the hunt for him again. And this particular species of shark tended to travel in schools ranging within the hundreds. The fact that he'd seen only three of them so far didn't mean that dozens more weren't lurking about nearby. The blood from their companion would draw more sharks and ignite their hunger. Despite the fact that the cutter was coming about, King knew they would never arrive in time to pull him from the water before the sharks renewed their hunt.

He sighed, raising his hands above the water to brush his tangled hair from his eyes. For the first time, he noticed the dried leathery texture of his skin—blackened from dehydration in a way similar to cured jerky meat. Though it was to be expected, the sight was still unnerving, to say the least. Like his hair and beard, his fingernails had grown to extraordinary lengths while he'd slept. He studied them closely. They were now at least two to three inches long, thick and yellowed with age. But despite his disgust at seeing his hands so ungroomed, the nails felt solid. Strong and healthy.

The fact that he could even see these details at all was testament to just how fast his vision, and thus his entire body, was being repaired. With this in mind, he turned his gaze toward the surface of the water, hoping to catch a glimpse of his face, but he was distracted by the sight of two sinewy bullets closing in on his treading form from below. The sharks, obviously finished with their cannibalistic meal, had resumed their pursuit.

It was time to finish this.

Taking a series of quick, shallow breathes followed by a single deep one, he dove headfirst back into the abyss, and swam directly toward his prey. While the sharks were faster and more maneuverable in the water, as well as immensely strong, cunning killers, King had one major advantage. Imagination. And he was more than prepared to use it.

The two hammerheads were now circling him, nearly fifteen feet below the surface, biding their time to strike. With their cephalofoil—the hammer-shaped head that gave them their namesake—King knew the creatures had an almost perfect three-hundred-and-sixty degree view of the aquatic landscape. There could be no sneaking up on them. No ambush from below or behind. And no weapons to be used against them even if he could find a way inside their field of vision. So, he stopped swimming, hovered patiently and waited.

One heartbeat. Two. Three. The shark to his right charged. Its eyes rolled back into its head as its maw stretch open and snapped. King twisted at the very last second, avoiding the attack. But his reprieve was only temporary. As he adjusted his spin, he caught sight of the second shark speeding toward him. This time, when he spun out of the way, his right hand grabbed hold of the creature's snout, and he was pulled through the water behind it. It bucked and thrashed, trying to throw him off, but King's grip held tight. If he let go now, it would be over. Maybe even permanently.

Taking a tighter hold around one of the eye-stalks, he drew himself closer to the beast until he managed to wrap one arm around the shark's neck. Its skin, comprised of thousands of toothy scales, sliced into his flesh as he slid across its back. Repositioning himself, he wrapped his legs around the hammerhead's tail, then flexed his free hand, and sent his long curved nails down near its spine. But its hide deflected the blow easily enough. He jabbed again with no effect. The third time, the nail of his index finger snapped off painfully, and he nearly lost his grip.

The shark, however, wasn't taking these blows lightly. With the third jab, it dove straight down, pulling King twenty, thirty, then fifty feet deep, and still descended. Its companion followed patiently, as if unwilling to risk injuring the other shark with a premature attack. Instead, it kept pace, its coal-black eye tracking every movement they made toward the ocean floor.

And with every foot they descended, King felt an aching pressure building on the inside of his chest wall. He wasn't certain, but he imagined he was nearly a hundred feet deep, and still being pulled down.

Realizing that an all-out·assault on the shark's back was futile, he chose to attack once more—this time along the beast's side, near its pectoral fin, where he hoped the armor would be weaker. Curling his fingers, he brought his arm around to the creature's side, and slid the nails underneath the scales and struck. The shark bucked beneath him before spiraling around in a desperate move to dislodge him. King's grip slipped, and he began falling away. But before the other shark could take advantage of the slip, he lashed out with his hand, and caught a handhold on something sponge-like. Fleshy. He glanced up to see his gnarled grip clutching at one of the hammerhead's gill slits. A small cloud of blood—evidence of damaged capillaries within the gills—plumed out from the slit as he squeezed.

Grinning, King pulled himself back up onto the shark's back with one hand, and pushed his other hand deeper into the gill. He probed the slit, slashing at the vulnerable viscera with his nails. He was rewarded by an even greater cloud of blood. The second shark, sensing its mate's billowing blood, quickly changed course. It zipped past King's head in an erratic motion. Sensing the fight was nearly over, King pushed with all his strength until he broke past the shark's exposed muscle, and into its throat. From there, he tore and ripped at anything his fingers could grasp, until suddenly, the hammerhead bucked violently, sending King spiraling through the water.

Holding out his arms, he managed to stabilize himself, then hovered in the azure abyss and watched as the uninjured shark swept after its counterpart. It crunched down on the other's tail, sending even more blood into the water, and then it began dragging its prey deeper toward the sea floor.

King watched for another moment, then kicked toward the surface with his one good leg. A few feet up, he could make out the long, curved form of the cutter's keel drifting directly above him.

Good, he thought, while continuing his ascent. *Now it's time to find out what all this is about.*

11

"No sign of 'im, Cap'n!" Leighfield cried, leaning over the port bow. He jumped as a clap of thunder cracked overhead, followed by a near-blinding streak of lightning. He whirled around to face Reardon and Finkle. "Yikes! Cap'n, how long you supposin' we need to keep lookin' for 'im? Surely those sharks got 'im, and the storm is nearly on top of us!"

Reardon glanced over at the old scientist. Finkle was uncertain how to answer the unspoken question from the captain. The one thing the Irishman had in common with his English quartermaster was that he hadn't liked the plan to seek out Lanme Wa from the very beginning. He'd thought it a complete waste of time. But Washington's, as well as his own influence had convinced Josiah Reardon's patron to accept the expedition's terms. The rewards had been just too good for the privateer's commander to pass up.

However, Finkle had seen the look in the captain's eyes when he had gazed upon the shriveled remains of the dead pirate. Rationally speaking, there was no reason to believe the man had actually been sleeping for nearly a century. The very idea was preposterous to any learned man.

But Finkle was convinced. He'd studied the legends. Scoured dozens of old documents spanning centuries. The pirate known as Lanme Wa had been around far longer than anyone guessed. The miracles that were attributed to him were beyond anyone's imagination to concoct, and Finkle knew without doubt that if the man was still alive, he was the only one who could lead this expedition to its prize.

"Just a while longer," Finkle said to the captain. "Give him a few moments more."

Reardon glanced over at the witch, who merely shrugged indifferently before saying, "Da man is truly as immortal as anyone can be, *mon capitaine*. I doubt a few toothy fish in da sea could do much to—"

"Witch!" Someone shouted from the stern of the ship. The voice was deep and guttural, as if each syllable had been sifted through a pile of wet, marble rubble. "I'll have words with you, witch!"

Everyone turned toward the quarterdeck to see the most ghastly of apparitions. Lanme Wa leaned against the rail, his back hunched down in fury...and possibly pain. His left leg was gone below the knee. Or was it? Finkle pushed his spectacles up onto his beak-like nose for a better look. There appeared to be the beginnings of a fetal foot growing from the already-healing tissue. Bone seemed to lengthen before their very eyes.

Winfield, the wheelman, leapt back with a cry at the sight. Now without hands to guide it, the wheel spun wildly to port, turning the ship back in the direction of the storm.

"Winfield!" Reardon shouted. The captain's eyes hadn't left the sight of the once-dead man crouching angrily on the deck of his ship. The wheelman, still keeping carefully out of reach of the newcomer, obediently took control of the wheel once more, and steered the ship back on course.

Finkle continued to stare at the man. His skin was still as black and leathery as when he'd first been dropped into the ocean, but now it glistened with moisture. It seemed to breathe on its own, as if it were taking on nutrients from the salty sea air to mend itself. Flesh, blood and bone mended together quickly, reforming the man as though God Himself were sculpting a new Adam from clay. The pirate's eyes were no longer cloudy, but instead were bright. Sharp. The irises as orange-brown as tanned leather. Long clumps of tangled hair hung down far past his shoulders, half-covering his face. But despite the obstruction, there could be no doubting the rage building within the man. Rage directed solely on the Creole mambo bokor.

For her part, the witch doctor took a single step back, then held her ground. She stared back at him defiantly, though she gripped the strap of her medicine bag tightly in her hands.

No one spoke. No one moved.

Finkle wondered if anyone had even taken a breath. But the pirate didn't seem to notice. His dark eyes were fixed on the witch as he took a single step from the rail, and came down on a perfectly formed, non-mummified foot that hadn't been there a moment before.

"Asherah," he growled. He spoke in an archaic form of French that Finkle could barely translate. "Perhaps you'll be so kind as to explain what's happening here."

The mambo bokor swallowed. She tried to pull her own eyes up from the deck to look at him, but she didn't seem to have the strength to do it. When she opened her mouth to speak, Lanme Wa interrupted.

"You see, I thought I'd made a deal with your grand-mother. I wasn't to be disturbed. Not until I either awoke on my own or..." The man's death's-head face appeared to be mending itself even as he spoke. The ghastly grin was already beginning to slip away behind a veil of flesh-like lips, making his words more articulate, if not menacing. "Or after three hundred years had passed." He waved a bony finger around the ship. "This doesn't look like the end of the twentieth century to me, Asherah, now does it?"

"*Monsieur*, I..." The bokor took another step back as he approached, lumbering down the steps of the quarterdeck directly toward her. Water dripped from the rags of his clothes with each shamble. "It's just dat..."

"Begging your pardon, sir," Finkle said, stepping in between the grisly pirate and the witch. He spoke French, but wasn't sure he could match the older style well enough to explain. Still, he had to try. "I'm afraid it's actually my fault that your slumber has been interrupted."

Lanme Wa stopped mid-stride, and turned to look at him. Finkle's heart thumped against his rib cage at the dark stare, but he managed to hold his ground. "You see, we're on an expedition. A search for something absolutely mindboggling, actually, and perhaps our only means of beating back the British from our land. From my research, I came to believe you were the only one on Earth able to guide us to our prize."

The man stared at Finkle, and cocked his head as if confused. "I know you." This time, the pirate spoke in a strange dialect of English the old scientist had never heard before.

"No. No, I don't think you do." Finkle cleared his throat nervously. "Jim Brannan Finkle's the name. At your service." He gave a quick, polite bow.

The pirate, his attention no longer on the bokor, stepped toward the old scientist. "No, that's not your name." He rubbed a long, thin finger across his brow. "It'll come to me, but I do know you."

"I don't know how that's possib—"

Thunder boomed overhead, nearly simultaneously with a blazing trail of lightning streaking through the sky.

"Gentleman," Josiah Reardon said, approaching Lanme Wa cautiously. "There'll be time for explanations later. For now, we need to navigate around this storm, and to do that, we need ye, Cap'n, to grant us safe passage past your ship."

The pirate glanced to the bow, a grim indecipherable smile spreading across his face.

His new lips are working well for him, Finkle thought.

"Just sail past them," the pirate said. "They won't attack. All they'll do is slowly trail you, giving you a wide berth."

"What?" Reardon asked.

"It's their nature, Captain. They're patient. Slow to act, unless provoked. Plus, they'll still be following my orders."

"And those were?"

"Should anyone abscond with me, they were to follow and see what manner of mischief laid about. Then, after discerning what my grave robbers had in mind, they could act." He nodded past the port bow. "At the moment, they're simply watching. They'll not attack 'til they're sure."

Reardon stared incredulously at his guest, then looked past the man's ever-broadening shoulders. "Winfield! Set course around that ship!" He spun around. "All hands to battle stations! Needles! Keep yer eyes fixed on that frigate!"

"Aye!"

The deck of the ship erupted in a blur of activity as the crew saw to their captain's orders. The rain was already starting to come down. If not for the pitch coating the deck's planks, at least two of the crew would have been swept overboard as the ocean beneath them began to swell.

"Cap'n, would ye care to join me at the wheel?" Reardon asked Lanme Wa. The Irish captain was putting on a good show of not appearing intimidated in the slightest by the pirate's cadaverous appearance.

Lanme Wa only nodded his assent, then followed Josiah Reardon up onto the quarterdeck and to the wheel. Relieving Winfield of his post, Captain Reardon gripped the wheel, and steered around an oncoming swell, making his way steadily toward the *Presley's Hound.*

Finkle was watching this when he sensed someone slide up next to him. "He doesn't seem to like you very much," he said to the vodou bokor.

"I am sure he's just disoriented from his long sleep, *cher.*"

"Or, perhaps, he's a good judge of character." The old man turned to look at her and found her emerald eyes burning with contempt. "Strike a nerve, did I?"

"Lanme Wa definitely be a good judge of character." She sniffed while clutching her bag more tightly. Her mop of unruly hair was now soaked from the sudden downpour, only helping to intensify her wild countenance. "I'd say you best be on your own guard 'bout dat. Make sure your *own* character is shiny 'nough to make da cut."

He wasn't sure what to make of her comment, so he ignored it, and moved on to the question he really wanted to know. "Can we trust him?"

She wiped the rainwater from her forehead with one hand, then grabbed hold of a rope to steady herself against a sudden lurch of the ship. She stood silently for a moment, then shrugged. "He'll do what is right by his reckoning, I s'pose. But don't cross him—*or me*—or you might just regret it."

Finkle turned back to the port side rail, and watched as they carefully sailed past the gray sails of the pirate ship a mere two hundred yards away. As Lanme Wa had predicted, the *Hound,* its deck lifeless and devoid of crew, let them pass without incident, and soon the crew of the

Reardon's Mark were moving out of the storm, and heading directly for the mysterious shores of Florida.

12

"It's time you explain yourselves," King said, pushing his cleaned plate away. He leaned back in his chair, and looked up at his three hosts sitting around the captain's table.

Captain Reardon, Quartermaster Greer and Finkle stared back at him with wide wonder-filled eyes, no doubt mesmerized by the speed with which his body was mending itself. Already, the hard mummified leather of his flesh was being replaced by the more supple skin and muscle of a living person. His leg was completely whole once more. His hands were free of scars. And though he hadn't seen his reflection in more than a hundred years, he imagined his face was already beginning to resemble that of Jack Sigler once more—or at least, it would, once he had a chance for a proper bath and a shave.

King drank from his cup of rum, savoring the warmth spreading through his body after the first full meal he'd had since his hibernation. Though the food had been bland, and the bread stale and filled with grubs, he'd enjoyed every bite more than he could remember of any meal before. However, now was the time to finally get to the bottom of all this. Time to find out why he'd suddenly awakened submerged in the Atlantic Ocean, attacked by a trio of hammerhead sharks.

He turned his attention on the older man of the group. Finkle felt so familiar to him, but the man had been right when he said there was no way the two could have possibly met before. King had sequestered himself to the grave thirty years before the old man had even been born. Maybe more. But his round face and high forehead were just so...familiar. There was something about the man's name that struck a chord as well. But that was the least of his concerns for the moment, so he shelved the thoughts for a later time. He repeated the question directly to the scientist, who seemed to be in charge of the expedition.

"Mr. Finkle? How about you? Please explain what this is all about."

Slowly, Finkle tore a piece of meat from a chicken leg, and chewed while he pondered the question. He then set the leg down, swallowed and leaned forward, putting his elbows on the table.

"Well now, that's all a bit complicated..."

"I'm a fast learner." King slammed a fist down on the table. "Mr. Finkle, you woke me prematurely. You stole me from my protective bed. You attempted to drown me...or feed me to the sharks. Don't play me for a fool. I suggest you stop beating around the bush and get to it."

"Yes, I understand completely." Nervously, the man took a sip of his wine, washing the remaining chicken down, then cleared his throat. His obvious trepidation seemed so ill-fitting for the man. Like a suit two sizes too small. King guessed Finkle—whoever he really was—was not someone who frightened easily, nor was one usually at a loss for words. "It's like this, Mister...I'm sorry. I'm not quite sure what to call you."

"I was born Jack Sigler. You can call me that if you'd like." Though most of the years he'd been wandering the world, he'd used pseudonyms or names given to him, he'd stopped really trying to hide his true identity a long time ago. At first, it had been a matter of protecting the time stream—of not inadvertently doing something that would change future events. The longer he'd lived, though, the more King realized that nothing he did ever truly managed to change anything. No matter how much he tried...no matter what evil despot he attempted to overthrow or well-known tragedy he fought to avert...nothing changed. He soon came to realize that history was fixed, and nothing he did would change the outcome, because he had always been a part of it. That included using his real name when the time called for it.

"Ah, Mr. Sigler...a German name, is it not?" Finkle asked with a delighted smile. "I thought I detected a slightly Germanic accent in your tongue."

"I've developed a few accents in my travels, Mr. Finkle. Now get on with it."

"Oh, yes. You see, Mr. Sigler, we are on a very important mission for the Continental Army." He paused, then cocked his head briefly. "No, no, no. This won't do. I forgot you've been asleep for so long. I'm sure you're familiar with America...the colonies of Britain... Well, we are..."

"I'm familiar with the colonial Revolution, Mr. Finkle." As King's body regenerated, so did his mind and the memories of his many pasts with it, including the names of those most dear to him at last: Fiona and Sara.

The three other men at the table gawked at the response.

"Y-you are?" Finkle asked. "But how? If you've slumbered for so long, then how could you possibly..."

"Just trust me on this. I'm very familiar with the uprising in America. With George Washington. And with..."

King allowed himself a smile as he gazed at the old man. "And you. *That's* where I know you from." He chuckled while doing a few mental calculations. "*Jim Brannan Finkle.* Very clever, that. But then what should I expect from you?"

Finkle looked at his two companions nervously, cleared his throat and fiddled with the cravat adorning his neck. "I'm sure I don't know what you're talking about, sir."

King leaned back further in his chair, and confidently kicked his feet up onto the table. "Don't worry, old man. Your secret is safe with me." King couldn't help himself. The realization had utterly changed his attitude toward the man. Where before, he'd been irked by the premature release from his tomb, now he found himself fascinated. Perhaps a little awestruck. "Now go on. Tell me."

Finkle nodded. "It's a race, actually, and we're losing. The British are searching for a place of immense power. Power enough to turn the tide of our rebellion as easily as one might shoo a fly. Power enough for them to spread their empire over the very face of the Earth."

King swung his feet off the table, and sat up. Interested. Though his memory of history was fading from the long years of living it, he didn't believe there'd been any recorded event where the British forces had discovered anything remotely as powerful as Finkle claimed. But that didn't mean the threat wasn't there.

"What kind of power?"

Finkle narrowed his eyes, then gave him a nervous once over. "Immortality."

13

They stepped from the captain's dining room, through the crew's quarters and up on deck where they were greeted by the sight of billions of stars in the heavens. They'd managed to skirt the storm with minimal damage to the cutter, and were now moving at a fast clip in a northwesterly direction. The ship rocked back and forth, as it sliced through the last remaining chop of the foul weather.

"Florida," Finkle said, as they strode up to the bow and gazed past the bowsprit. "We're heading to Florida."

King glanced back, peering into the darkness at the sea behind them. Though they would sail without lights, he knew without question that the stalwart and unearthly crew of the *Presley's Hound* was not too far away. A twinge of guilt cut into his chest at the thought of those poor souls waiting so patiently for him to emerge from his...for lack of a better word...melancholy. They'd endured so much. Suffered so many cruelties before he'd freed them from their horrific bondage. The one who'd done the horrible things to them had seen them as little more than pack animals. Servants. Easily disposable. King had never been able to tolerate it, so when the opportunity came, he'd set a contingent of them free, and they had been loyal to him ever since.

"...are you listening, Mr. Sigler?" Finkle's soft, even-keeled voice eased him back to the present.

"Sorry. What were you saying?"

"A recently discovered document from Ponce de Leon has surfaced. The British managed to procure it before our spies could get their hands on it, but our people did manage to copy most of it down. The document traces a path deep into the Florida jungles to where a fount of..."

"Let me stop you right there. First, the reason the Spaniards assumed the Fountain of Youth—that *is* what you're talking about, right? The Fountain of Youth?" Finkle gave a slight nod in response. "Right. The only reason the Spaniards thought it was actually in Florida was that the common height of the European male back in the fifteenth century was less than five feet tall. The Native...um, the Indians, averaged more than six feet tall. The Spaniards had heard rumors about the Fountain since Columbus stumbled there. They mistranslated. Thought the Caribe Indian word for 'Life' meant 'Youth' instead. So, the taller humans must certainly have drunk from a fountain that bestowed more... *life*. More body mass."

"But..."

"Second, Ponce de Leon, despite popular misconceptions and legends, never sought the Fountain. I know, because I was with him for much of his expedition to the New World. As far as I know, he never got a chance to search for it. He was too preoccupied with gaining new territory for the Spanish Crown."

"Oh, please," Quartermaster Greer scoffed. "Do you really expect us to believe that you are nearly three hundred years old? You must be, if you really sailed with Juan Ponce de Leon, and I, for one, cannot possibly give credence to..."

"Greer!" Reardon shouted. "Stand down."

"But, sir!"

"I said, stand down, Mr. Greer, or I'll assign ye to the galley for the remainder of the evening."

"My apologies for the interruption, Mr. Sigler," Finkle said. "And while I, too, am utterly fascinated by the prospect that you are as old as your comment implies, I'll respect your privacy on the matter, and proceed with our discussion." He glared at Greer to be sure the man wasn't about to interrupt again before continuing. "Bear in mind, though, I never said the document in question even had anything to do with Ponce de Leon himself—only that it was supposedly in his possession."

This stopped King in his tracks. "What?"

King was perplexed. He'd sailed with the man. Intentionally. Ever since being tricked into drinking the elixir that had made him near immortal, he'd scoured the Earth for any legends having to do with the subject of longevity, in hopes of better understanding his condition. Like most twentieth century people, he'd been led to believe that Ponce de Leon was a great explorer who came to the New World in search of the legendary fount. But it simply wasn't true. Ponce de Leon, by then the governor of Hispania, had merely traveled to Florida to expand Spain's empire. His expedition had been political in nature, and not the legendary adventure most people imagined.

"I said the document wasn't penned by the famed explorer, Mr. Sigler. But rather by a Spanish soldier named Phillipe Guerrera, who'd become lost, deep in the jungles. Seems the young man had been on a scouting party. His group had been betrayed by one of their Mayaca Indian guides and led into an ambush. These Indians killed everyone in the scouting party, but Guerrera managed to survive by crawling along the ground into a stand of nearby palmetto bushes. He was later found, injured and nearly dead of dehydration, by a Mayacan hunter. He was taken deep into the jungle by way of the St. Johns River—then known as *Rio de Corientes* —until they came to the hunter's village."

King shook his head. "This makes no sense. I'm aware of the Mayacans. They were hunter-gatherers..." His three hosts seemed to cock their heads simultaneously in confusion, unfamiliar with the anthropological term. "They weren't violent. Just wanted to live in peace and take care of their tribe."

"Perhaps you're right," Finkle said. "But just hear me out. The story itself may provide the answers to your conundrum." With a gesture from King, the old man continued. "Guerrera was nursed back to health, only to be forced into a strange type of slave labor."

"Why do you call it 'strange?'"

"Because it wasn't your typical manual labor they forced upon him, Mr. Sigler. It was something far more macabre. You see, the village seemed to have an incredibly high mortality rate. At the same time, Mr. Guerrera noted, their numbers never seemed to ebb. He soon discovered the reason. When they deemed him healthy enough, they set him to his dark labors—carrying the bodies of the dead to a specific point along the St. Johns River. He would then set up some sort of ritualistic tableau around the cadavers, and leave."

"Funerary work," King said. "Not so unusual with these cultures. They have deep superstitions concerning the dead. Makes sense they'd risk a strange white man's life for such..."

"The next morning, these former corpses would be back within the village. Walking. Talking. Sharing with the community."

King, who'd been listening carefully, while gazing at the churning water of the Atlantic, spun around. "What?"

"Precisely my reaction when I first read the pilfered account," Finkle chuckled. "But there was something most definitely wrong with these seemingly resurrected individuals, according to Guerrera. They were indeed there. They were seen by all. But they were hardly tangible."

"Ghosts? Are you talking about ghosts?"

"Guerrera denies that. His words are literally translated as 'Shades of Matter.' They were, as I said, *hardly* tangible...but his account seems to indicate they were indeed tangible on some level. They could touch and be touched. They could affect the environment around them, brandish tools and weapons and even sate their own basest of carnal needs. As a matter of fact, there seemed to even be rites where their shaman practiced this with some regularity with the female Shades." Finkle blushed at this, then shook his head apologetically. "But I'm getting carried away. The fact is, something within that Floridian jungle brought those people back to life. Guerrera guessed it had something to do with a small tributary of the river, where those funerary rites, as you called them, were carried out. He believed he'd stumbled upon the famed fountain for which adventurers had been searching for centuries."

King stared in silence for several long moments, then laughed. "That's it? That's all you have to go on? Ghost stories?"

"That's precisely why we went in search of you, lad," Reardon said, scowling. "The professor here believed ye had found the fountain as well. The reason for yer 'unnatural longevity,' he called it."

King glanced at Finkle, then back to the captain. "Well, he's wrong. My condition was caused by...by something else entirely." He stared out into the night, tracing the gentle silver stripes of the moon's reflection over the water. "So you can take me back. Now. To resume my sleep. I have no business here, in this time."

"But..."

"Take me back!" He wheeled around on Reardon, his eyes burning with anger. "Or I will call to my crew, and they will take your ship by force. And trust me, Captain, that's *not* something you want to ever endure."

"I don't take kindly to threats, *sir*. I've half a mind—"

"Half a mind is right," Finkle broke in. "Captain Reardon, please walk away, and let me discuss our options with Mr. Sigler here, if you please."

Reardon glared at the old man, ground his teeth, then spun on his heels and stormed off toward the quarterdeck.

"Forgive him, Captain Sigler. He's a good man, but he wanted no part in retrieving you to begin with. I'm afraid, that little misadventure was entirely my fault," Finkle continued with a tilt of his head. "Now, you threaten to hinder our mission's timeline even further by insisting we take you back, and that's not something this crew can afford."

"Then my own crew can bear that burden, and yours can be on their way toward your little pipe dream."

"Pipe...er, dream?"

"Never mind. Just an expression. Simply put, it just means it's completely futile. A fairy tale. I've traveled the world in search of these legends of immortality, and none of them have ever panned out. Human immortality is just not something that can be found." He paused before looking up at the stars. "At least, not in nature anyway."

Finkle edged up to the rail, and looked out over the ocean. He withdrew a pipe from his coat, lit it and proceeded to smoke silently for several minutes. After a while, he exhaled a ring of gray smoke into the air and looked over at King.

"I realize it's none of my business, but I'm curious... what exactly happened to you?"

King cocked his head. "I'm not sure what you mean."

"Well, I'm just trying to figure out what drives a man to hide away from the world in a grave." Finkle pointed out at the ocean with the stem of his pipe. "With all the beauty this world has to offer...with the mysteries it continues to conceal...with all there is to experience, why on Earth would someone wish away his life like you have?"

"You have no idea what it's like to live as long as—"

"Your longevity is not the issue here, and you know it. Look, you may have everyone else fooled, but not me. You're no pirate. Stories of your voyages are rife with tales of piracy, but you never once acted the part. You were never a cutthroat. Never killed for the sake of killing. And the only ships you ever concerned yourself with were slave ships. You'd take their cargo, and the slaves were said to be set free on several uncharted islands along the Caribbean. Islands in which you helped establish permanent settlements. That isn't the act of a pirate."

"Your point is?"

"The point is, Captain Sigler, that it takes something mighty devastating to make a good man crave death over life, and I would sort of like to know—"

"Argh!" Someone screamed near the stern of the ship, followed immediately by the clap of a pistol being fired.

King and Finkle wheeled around to see Captain Reardon grappling with a shadowy form near the wheel. Two more shadows slithered over the railing and onto the quarterdeck. They lunged at three sailors running to help their captain.

Finkle leaned forward, preparing to assist as well, but he was stopped by King's strong hand against his chest. "No," he said quietly. "They'll take one, and only one."

"What? What are you saying?"

King took a step forward and barked out an indecipherable order. The three shadows quickly stopped their assault. Their faces, covered by black fraying hoods, stared back at him. Their hissing, wheezing gasps of understanding could barely be heard over the sea winds. Then, without warning, they seized the sailor closest to the rail and disappeared over the side with their prize.

14

"What, pray tell, were those things?" Captain Reardon shouted, as he rushed over to Sigler. "You gave one command, and they obeyed you without question! What devilry did ye bring aboard my ship?"

Jack Sigler, who stood a full foot and a half taller than the captain, stared down at him with a face of stone.

"Captain, I'm sure there's a perfectly reasonable explanation for this," Finkle said. He could tell the hotheaded Irishman was about to do something rash. Something he'd ultimately regret. "We just need to calm down, and I'm certain Captain Sigler will explain what just happened."

Sigler turned from Reardon to Finkle, and shrugged. "I just saved the lives of your crew, gentlemen. Those creatures came here to feast. I only allowed them a small taste." As if this was enough, the pirate began striding toward the hatch leading to the living quarters of the ship. "Now, I'm going to get myself cleaned up, and think about all you've told me, Mr. F...er, Finkle. For now, you can continue course to Florida. I'm not saying I'll help you, but I am intrigued enough to consider it."

As the ancient pirate descended into the hold, Finkle couldn't help but breathe a relieved sigh. There was something very dark in this strange man, who seemed older by far than even the tales indicated. But the darkness felt alien to him. Somehow Finkle knew, it just didn't belong. It was, he believed, a darkness born of great sorrow, and despite the man's flippant manner in regard to the life of the unfortunate sailor, Finkle feared the great Lanme Wa would only add his death to a mountain of sins that would fester in the man's soul, unless something could be done about it.

"So, you still believe havin' that abomination on board is a good idea, boyo?" Reardon growled into Finkle's ear. "'Cause I'm havin' some serious doubts at the moment."

The old man kept his eyes trained on the hatch that Sigler had just descended, and shook his head. "I do. What's more, I believe, though he may not know it yet, he needs to be part of this expedition for his own sake. No, we proceed as planned." He then looked at the captain. "But I'd probably consider doubling the watch for the remainder of our voyage, if I were you."

King sat back in the bunk with a sigh. He'd commandeered the captain's personal quarters. Had helped himself to the water basin to wash himself off as best he could, then shaved. He had finally begun to feel a modicum of himself again, except for the slight thumping of his heart against his chest.

He hadn't expected the hunting party. Hadn't called *them*. Hadn't planned on any of Captain Reardon's crew being molested by them, while he had any say in the matter. Yet, against his wishes, they'd slipped on board and were now responsible for the death of an innocent man. For the first time since his awakening, he feared for his crew. What had the century without his guidance done to them? What had they fed on? Did they starve while they awaited his return, and now, famished, were they unable to repress their baser instincts?

If that was the case, this expedition—on their fool's errand—was doomed. Unless he could find a mutually beneficial means of dealing with the problem. But he wouldn't know that until he had a chance to reunite with the *Presley's Hound* and see his crew's state of mind firsthand.

So that's what you'll do then. Tomorrow, at day break, you'll take a little swim over to the Hound *and see for yourself.*

There was a tap at his door, breaking him from his thoughts.

"Yes?"

"*Monsieur* Lanme Wa?" The voice behind the door was Asherah's. "May I come in?"

King restrained himself from growling irritably, and opted to roll his eyes instead before answering. "You may."

The door cracked open, and Asherah's large green eyes peeked around the corner at him. Trepidation and humility radiated from them. King felt the Creole woman was quite the actress.

"Lanme Wa, I've come to offer you my most sincere apologies." He waved her further inside, and she complied, closing the door behind her. From the oil lamp burning in the corner of the room, he could make out her firm, slender form underneath the cotton fabric of her dress. Sweat glistened off her bare shoulders, and ran down her neck toward the valley of her two breasts. When he looked up into her eyes, he caught the briefest of smiles on her face. She'd caught him noticing, and obviously enjoyed it. "I be truly sorry. I've done dishonored both you and my grandmamma. But when dey came to da island, I didn't know what to do. Dere were so many of 'em. Wit' guns. Dey were goin' to take you, whether I liked it or not, so I made dem take me along. To protect you how I could." She moved over to the bunk in which he was lounging, leaned forward and gently traced her fingertips across his bare chest. Her eyes stared into his with a lustful hunger. "I'm here for you. Your servant."

Faster than humanly possible, his right hand shot out, grabbing her by the wrist, and he shoved her away in disgust.

"Don't mistake me for a fool, witch." He sat up, whipping his legs over the edge of the bed, and planting his feet on the floor. "You can't charm me with your wiles, the same way you can the others aboard this ship. And I won't be played. Remember, I've known you, your entire life. And I know what you did."

Her eyes widened at this revelation. "*Monsieur?* How do you know dis?" King detected the slightest of tremors in her voice, a far cry from the confident vixen she'd been upon entering his cabin.

King snarled a derisive laugh. "You've been 'serving' me from the time you were first able to walk. Feeding me. Watching me. And all that time, I was, in a manner of speaking, watching *you* as well. Most of the time, it was unconsciously, but I was paying attention. I observed you grow up. I felt the selfishness and greed well up inside you." He stood up and stalked over to her, backing her into the corner of the room. "And I *heard* you, too."

With a nervous gulp, she made the sign of the cross with her right hand. "H-heard me?"

Feeling his anger rise like bile into his throat, King growled and lashed out at her, grasping her by the neck and giving a gentle, but stern squeeze. "Heard you kill her. Heard you murder your own grandmother. Heard you declare yourself the next Asherah."

At this, King felt her muscles relax. It was only the slightest of differences, but he felt it nonetheless. Whatever she'd been afraid he had discovered, this wasn't it. She didn't mind him knowing about the murder of her grandmother. No, there was something else she was keeping from him, and that unnerved him more than anything.

"Monsieur, I can't breathe." The witch's caramel-colored face was now an ashen gray, and her sultry, emerald eyes protruded from her skull, as she struggled to take in the simplest of breaths. King wondered if the world might not be a better place if he simply ended her life there, or at least forced her to tell him what she had planned. But something in the back of his mind railed against such an action. It was something that Lanme Wa might very well do, but not the man he once was. Not what Jack Sigler, callsign: King, would ever even contemplate.

Slowly, he eased his grip from around her throat, then stepped away. "You need to leave," he said, returning to his bunk. For several moments, she stood there, heaving for air while rubbing her bruised neck. Though obviously physically distressed, her expression was unreadable beyond that. If he'd made an even worse enemy in his actions today, she wasn't going to let him know it. "But before you go, know this: I'm watching you, witch. I'm not sure what's going on in that pretty little head of yours, but I won't offer my back to you the way your grandmother did. Mark my words on that."

After a few more labored breaths, Asherah straightened, sniffed at the air and moved toward the door. When she opened it, she paused. "You can watch me all you want, *monsieur.*" She turned to face King with her familiar alluring smile. "I love da thought of dose delicious eyes on me. But understand something. You may know me, but I know *you* just as well. Though you have great strength and skill in battle...though you seemingly cannot die...you still are just a man, in da end. A sealed tomb kept you in a prison of your own making. Others might know ways of doin' da same."

Before he could respond, she gave a curt nod of her head and slipped out of the cabin, closing the door behind her.

15

Twenty Miles Off the Florida Coast
Two Days Later

An unseasonably chill wind whipped against King's face as he climbed onto the main deck. A blanket of dark clouds blotted out the night sky and the pale illumination from the quarter moon. The moment he materialized on deck, he was accosted by a slight, redheaded sailor running up to greet him.

"Master Sigler," the sailor said. His eyes wouldn't quite look King in the face. "Master Finkle needs to see ye on the fo'castle immediately, sir. If'n ye don't mind that is."

"Is there a problem?"

"Don't rightly know, sir. Just sent me to fetch ye, sir."

Without another word, King strode toward the bow of the ship, and took the three steps up to the forecastle deck in a single bound. Finkle stood next to a chart table with a sextant in hand. A lantern swayed back and forth above the map resting on the table, making it difficult to see much with any real clarity. When Finkle heard King's approach, he turned and greeted him with a sober nod.

"It's a bit late for you to be up charting our course, isn't it?" King said to the man. It was approaching the third watch of the night. The captain and most of the crew had long since retired for the night. Now, only a skeleton crew remained on deck.

"I'll sleep when our expedition is at an end. We'll be in Florida by mid-morning," he said.

"You don't look very happy about that."

The scientist shook his head. "We've got a problem. Needles, our lookout, spotted sails a few miles west of us, just before dusk. It was too far away to identify its colors, and now that it's dark, there's no way to know where it is in order to avoid it."

King pondered this for a moment. "This is a privateer vessel, right?"

Finkle nodded.

"So it's been given letters of marque."

"I'm not sure where you're going with this."

"Simple. As a privateer, you're not required to hoist American colors. You could, for example, hoist the Union Jack, if you'd like. Or the Spanish flag. If the ship out there is an enemy, make sure you're their friend when you sail past."

"But that's..."

"What? Unfair? Dishonest? That's one of the major advantages of employing a privateer. Guerrilla naval tactics, if you will."

"What kind of naval tactics?" Finkle asked, confused.

"Nevermind. I say you use every advantage you have, considering the size and armament of a ship this small." He smiled at the round old man. "It's how I was going to suggest sailing into St. Augustine. The British currently are in possession of it, if my history's correct, right?"

"Yes, they are," Finkle said, then cocked his head. "History?"

"Point is, we need a plan to get into Matanzas Bay, and a British flag will do just that. Do we have any spare canvas aboard to fabricate one?"

Finkle nodded. "I believe so. I'm just uncertain whether Captain Reardon is going to be particularly open to any of your suggestions at the moment." He leaned against the rail near the bowsprit and sighed. "Truth is, that attack by those creatures the other day has him even more wary of you than he was before. He doesn't think we should trust you."

"And what do you think?"

The old man shrugged. "By your own admission, you're not exactly committed to this expedition. Furthermore, you *are* a pirate, after all...no matter how much I'd like to think otherwise." He shook his head. "I honestly don't know. What *should* I think, Captain Sigler? You haven't exactly been forthcoming with me."

"And why should I be? You abducted me. I was satisfied where I was. Not harming anyone. Letting time pass me by in peace, and you ripped me away from that without so much as a 'please' and 'thank you.' For all intents and purposes, I'm a prisoner on board this ship...albeit a far-from-helpless one."

"I'm truly sorry about that," Finkle said. From the tone of the man's voice, King believed him. "But I honestly felt I had no choice. I believe in what we are trying to do with this revolution. I believe in everything our nation stands for, and this belief drives my every action. So I guess a better question to ask you is, what is it that you believe in? Answer that, and I'll know exactly if I should trust you or not."

"I'm not sure I believe in anything anymore."

"Really?" Finkle said. His voice was a mere whisper of amazement. "I've lived for seven decades, and not once have I ever met a man who believed in nothing at all." He chuckled. "As a matter of fact, I'm not sure I believe that it's even possible to not believe in at least one thing in this world."

King leaned against the rail next to Finkle. He had no obligation to the old scientist. Had no reason to even consider helping him. From his experience, King knew that the Revolution would be fought. The Americans would defeat the British, and the United States would prosper. No matter what he did, that much wouldn't change. Of course, there was also the undeniable fact that perhaps the Continental Army's victory over the British was a direct result of his own participation. But if that was the case, then there was hardly a decision to be made at all. He either would or wouldn't get involved, depending on how history originally played out.

It was all so confusing. Even after living thousands of years...after experiencing victory and defeat so many times...he still wasn't entirely sure how it worked. But in the end, he knew, he still wasn't obligated to win over this little man. Or the captain, for that matter. The problem was, there was something—he couldn't quite explain it— deep inside him that wanted this man's approval. Wanted this man's acceptance of him. Finkle, or whatever he chose to call himself, was a great man. Someone that King had looked up to since childhood. He needed this hero to like him. To see him as he truly was. If only King could remember just what that man really looked like.

"I...I believe in this," King finally said, reaching inside his shirt and withdrawing a metal chain with a small metal pin attached to it. "And the promise it represents. The promise to stop an evil man, no matter what it takes."

"Sounds like revenge to me," Finkle said. "Not sure that's a wise standard on which to build any trust."

King nodded. "It's not so much revenge, though. It's my mission. And it's essential to saving the world...somehow." While the major players of his future history lingered at the fringes of his long memory, the details had grown vague, like looking through fogged glass. He slipped the pendant-like pin back into his shirt. "But when I think about it, that's only part of it. I keep that thing around my neck to remind me of what's at stake when I return home. I can't always remember the details, but I definitely know the stakes." King turned to look at Finkle. "The two women of my life. My fiancée and my daughter. They're who I fight for. They're who I've survived all this time for, and the reason I hid myself away in a grave."

"Ah, now *love* is something I can fully support." Finkle gave a sad smile. "But why live in death because of it? I don't understand."

Before King could answer, there was a cry of alarm from the main deck. The two men wheeled around to see six black-clad figures climbing over the port side. Another eight scrambled over the starboard rails, and immediately set to work barring the hatches leading down to the sleeping quarters, then skewering the few crew members still on the main deck with cutlasses.

"Boarding party!" Needles shouted from the crow's nest. "To arms! To arms!" Instantly, the clattering of an alarm bell could be heard from all over the ship, followed by the sound of surprised men being shaken from their sleep. With the hatches barred from the outside, however, reinforcements wouldn't come anytime soon.

"Are these your men again?" Finkle asked, but King was already bounding down the steps, running unarmed into battle. "I suppose not."

The boarding party wore dark colors, helping them blend into the night and making it impossible to tell their nationality or purpose. But since the Golden Age of Piracy was long gone and the ship was so close to British-controlled waters, King guessed these were British forces and not pirates. They'd obviously approached in long boats under the cover of darkness, which meant their ship was somewhere nearby, ready to fire their cannons and scuttle the *Reardon's Mark* if these men were unable to commandeer it.

King veered for the nearest boarder, who had just impaled one of the *Mark's* crew with a sword. He slipped in from behind, wrapped one arm around the man's head and gave a swift jerk. The man's neck snapped with ease, and his boots clattered on the deck, drawing the attention of two of his companions. They raised their pistols and prepared to fire.

Still holding on to the dead boarder with one arm, King spun around, letting the momentum hurl the corpse at his attacker on the left while leaping toward the one on his right. Before the man could fire, King crouched low, lashing out with a sweeping kick that took the assailant's legs out from under him. In the same motion, King slipped a dagger from his boot, rolled forward and sliced the man's throat with a flick of his wrist. A bubbling fount of crimson surged up from the jagged slit.

King's vicious assault had garnered the attention of the entire boarding party, and they began converging on him with weapons drawn. Several had flintlock pistols trained at him, while the rest stood back, their cutlasses raised in the air. A slow steady rage began to boil from somewhere deep inside King's chest. He was tired of fighting. Just so tired of everything. For nearly three thousand years he'd been enduring one fight after another. All he wanted to do was be left alone. To sleep out the remaining years until he could once more be with the two people that were all the world to him. But no matter how hard he tried...no matter how far he ran...they always found him. Always threatened him. Always forced him to act. And he was sick of it.

Then he noticed one of the boarders slowly shift, bringing his pistol around to bare on Finkle. King was suddenly hit with a gut-wrenching realization. Something inside him clicked. Crouched down next to the body of the bleeding boarder, he let out a low growl of warning. His brow furrowed as every muscle in his body tensed. He wanted to tear each of these men apart, limb from limb, but he would give them one last chance to flee. It was taking every ounce of strength he had just to hold off his wrath.

Then, it happened. The one pointing his weapon at the old man pulled back the hammer of his pistol with a slow *click-clack*. King roared, leapt into the air and forgot himself in the carnage that followed.

16

Jim Brannan Finkle stood upon the forecastle, his mouth slack, as he watched with bone-chilling fascination and dread. He'd never in his life seen any man move the way Lanme Wa—this Jack Sigler—did. Like a fluid wave of energy lashing out at one boarder after another. While in France, Finkle had been treated to a number of ballets that had left him mesmerized at just how versatile and fluid the human form could be. The poise and balance of the dancers had been the pinnacle of human physiological achievement in his mind...until this very moment. Now, the old man realized that those dancers had been little more than toddlers compared to the grace and agility of the predatory spirit that inhabited this supposedly immortal pirate. Finkle shuddered to think what would happen if the pirate's gleaming fierce eyes turned their gaze to him and the crew of the *Reardon's Mark*.

The moment the pirate had leapt into the thick of battle, his motions had become a blur. Before actually meeting him, Finkle had supposed that centuries of life and war had nearly perfected the man's skills at killing. He had not been wrong.

In just under twenty-five seconds, with only a short dagger appropriated from his first victim, Jack Sigler had sliced his way through seven of the British sailors who had boarded the *Mark*. Five remained alive, and two now pulled the triggers of their flintlocks. With twin cracks, and two plumes of choking gray smoke, the pistol balls tore through Sigler's chest like drill bits boring into butter. Blood erupted like geysers from the two wounds, and Finkle found himself gasping at the sudden turn of fortune. But Sigler didn't collapse from the impacts. They didn't even slow him down. Instead, as the two boarders worked to reload their weapons with shaking hands, he hurled his dagger into the nearest shooter's chest and lunged at the second with a snarl. He grabbed the unfortunate man's neck with his hand and squeezed until his fingers punctured the throat with a sickening wet slurp.

Then, he dropped the dead man and spun around to size up the remaining three boarders. Blood-tinged saliva oozed from the pirate's lower lip as he heaved for breath; his shoulders hunched in preparation for another attack. But the opportunity never came. The three men, obviously terrified of the ferocity of this man who seemed so impervious to pistol balls, ran for the starboard rail and leapt into the placid sea below.

"That was...that was astonishing!" Finkle exclaimed.

Jack Sigler ignored the comment and dashed over to the starboard rail. Then, leaping over the bodies strewn along the deck, he ran to the port rail and leaned forward. After a moment, he pulled away and leapt up to the quarterdeck and took the wheel.

"Lower the main sails!" he shouted. "We're out of time!"

Finkle glanced around, waiting for the crew members to obey the pirate's orders. But there was no one left alive on deck. The few men on the main deck at the time of the attack lay in pools of their own blood. Needles still remained in the crow's nest, apparently too mortified by the carnage he'd just witnessed to utter a single syllable in response. Finkle could hear pounding at the three hatches that were still barred. The remainder of the crew were still below deck, oblivious to just what had transpired a few seconds before.

"Finkle! I said, lower the main sails! Now!" Sigler cried.

Gathering his wits, the scientist tottered down from the forecastle, and moved to the main mast, being careful not to step in any of the viscera painting the deck. After fumbling with the halyards for a few clumsy seconds, he managed to lower the sail to Sigler's satisfaction. A moment later, the entire ship turned about to the northeast. Finkle grabbed hold of one of the lines to keep from tipping over with the sudden turn, then ran to the central hatch and unlatched it. Immediately, it popped open and the crimson-faced Reardon exploded from below.

"What in blazes is happenin' up here?" he shouted, then he stopped in his tracks the moment he laid eyes on the corpses littering the deck. "Blessed Mary!"

"It's a long story. We were boarded. Captain Sigler took care of them, and now is..."

BOOM!

A crack of thunder erupted from somewhere to the west of them, followed by a blinding flash of light.

"Cannon fire!" Needles shouted.

There was a whistling sound that streaked toward them before plunging into the water just yards away from their bow.

"Battle stations!" Reardon cried. "Gunners to the carronades!"

Eight men rushed to the four short-barreled, smooth-bored, rotating cannons mounted to the bow, port and starboard of the ship, and prepared the weapons for firing.

Satisfied they were prepared, Reardon moved up to the quarterdeck with Finkle in tow.

"They're running without lanterns," Sigler said before the captain could question him. "Last spotted their ship on the port side, but they were coming about. I've managed to pull your ship out of range, but it looks like we're up against an old galleon. They easily outgun us."

"Then we've no choice," Reardon said. His face was grim and pale in the dim light of the cloud-hidden moon. "We'll have to outrun them."

"How would you like to do that? They're running three shrouds. We've only got the two. They'll catch us in no time."

The Irishman let out an indecipherable curse. "Then we have to stand our ground."

Sigler smiled at this. Finkle couldn't quite decide if it was out of sincere mirth or something more maniacal.

"That's the first thing you've said since I've awakened that makes me kind of like you, buddy," Sigler said.

"Buddy?"

"Never mind. But it won't come down to us fighting it out with them." He nodded off to his left. "Remember, I've got my own crew."

Finkle and Reardon turned in the direction he indicated to see the silhouette of the immense frigate, the *Presley's Hound*, coming alongside them and blocking any further cannon fire that might stray their way.

"They're mad!" Reardon shouted. "Even a ship that size can't stand a full barrage of cannon fire for too long against a galleon. What are they thinking?"

Sigler laughed. It was the first time Finkle had heard the sound come from his lips since they woke him, and this time, he got the distinct impression that it was one of genuine amusement.

"Three things, Captain." Sigler was beaming now. "First, my crew is extremely loyal to me. And second, like me, they're not exactly easy to kill."

"And the third thing?"

Though the roar of the wind and the flapping of sails was near deafening, the trio atop the quarterdeck began hearing something else in that particularly chill night— the sudden eruption of terrified screams from several hundred yards in the distance. One by one, another voice joined in the symphony of agonizing wails carried on the sea's winds from the enemy vessel.

"The third thing is that except for when I stopped them the other night, my crew hasn't fed in almost a century. They're famished, and that ship represents an all-you-can-eat buffet." He turned to face Reardon and Finkle, still smiling. "Now, I think it's safe. Let's go to Florida."

With that, he sailed past the *Presley's Hound*, corrected course to a more easterly direction, and set his eyes on the horizon.

17

St. Johns River Basin
Ninety-Two Miles Southwest of St. Augustine
Three Days Later

The rest of the trip had been relatively uneventful. However, because they'd been attacked at sea by a British vessel, it was generally regarded as a bad idea to attempt sailing into Matanzas Bay under the banner of any flag. Instead, they'd found a secluded lagoon several miles south of St. Augustine, and had set anchor with a regiment of sailors to guard the ship.

Now, the rest of the crew—totaling around twenty-three men—along with Sigler, the mambo bokor and Finkle, hacked at the heavy vines and undergrowth of the Florida jungle as they followed a small tributary of the St. Johns River.

"How much farther do you think the main river is?" Quartermaster Greer asked, dabbing at his brow with a handkerchief before swatting away a cloud of gnats. "These loathsome insects are maddening!"

Why did Reardon insist on bringing this limp-wristed fop along for the final leg of the expedition? Finkle rolled his eyes. He was nearly forty years the Englishman's senior, and even he was having an easier time navigating the dense vegetation than the younger sailor. "We'll get there when we get there," was the only reply he deigned to muster.

In hindsight, Finkle could hardly blame the man. They'd been trekking for the better part of three days with only a few brief stops to replenish their water, to eat from their poorly stocked rations and to catch a few hours' sleep at a time. Even though they were swiftly approaching nightfall, the heat was blistering. The humidity was even worse, sapping their strength as quickly as it sucked away the moisture in their bodies. Their clothes were thoroughly soaked from sweat, chafing the skin beneath like wet sandpaper. And if the gnats didn't pluck the flesh from their bones, the mosquitoes and vicious yellow flies certainly would. That was, if the voluminous alligators or snakes that haunted the basin didn't devour them first.

"Finkle," Sigler said, coming to a halt and bringing the company to a dead stop behind him. "Better check our notes." He glanced down at the compass in his hand. "We seem to be veering slightly off course."

Finkle squeezed past the line of men, surrounded entirely by stands of ancient cypress, their roots extending up from the ground like the legs of some spindly monstrous spiders. The illusion was complete when he crouched to pass under a low-lying branch and was brushed by the web-like fronds of Spanish moss that hung like ancient beards from the trees' limbs. Finally, he sidled up to Sigler, pulled his journal from his pack and opened it.

"Unfortunately, this section of Florida hasn't been well-explored," he mumbled, riffling through the pages.

"Not many trustworthy maps to choose from. All I had to go on were the pilfered pages of Guerrera's journal."

"I'm aware of that." Sigler took a drink from his water bladder. "But something tells me we're too far east. I think we need to move more inland."

Finkle's finger traced the poorly scrawled hand-written notes in his journal. He shook his head. "I don't understand. We should be dead on course. We've already passed several of the landmarks Guerrera wrote about. If the difference was due to land erosion, we'd be closer, not further away."

Sigler tapped the compass with his palm. "Okay. This is strange."

"What's going on?" Reardon asked, as he came up to them. His pale cheeks were rosy red from heat, and his Irish red hair was nearly dark brown from sweat.

"I'm not sure." Sigler tapped the compass again. "We seem to be in some sort of odd magnetic field. It's not pointing north." After a few more slaps with his palm, he sighed. "Look, it's getting dark. It'd be best to move on up until we can find a decent clearing and make camp. Then, I'll try to figure out what's wrong with the compass."

They agreed with his assessment, and within another forty-five minutes, they had set up camp in a small half-acre clearing next to the bank of the tributary. As the men worked to secure the camp, Sigler found a spot on an overturned tree and sat down to examine the compass. Finkle, feeling more in the way at the moment than anything, moved over to the pirate, pulled off his backpack and sat down.

"Any idea what's wrong with it?"

Sigler let out a soft chuckle. "You're the scientist. You tell me."

"I'm afraid I haven't dedicated much time to the science of magnetism." He lit his pipe and took in a deep puff. "Seems rather more a novelty than anything really useful. Just never been interested."

Sigler stopped and looked at the old man, a look of incredulity across his face. "This? Coming from you?" He shook his head in obvious amusement. "You'd be amazed at how much magnetism goes along with the other research you've done."

"Really? Do tell."

"Sorry, Professor. Space-time continuum and all that."

"You have the strangest speech patterns, my boy. Most of the time, I have no idea what you're going on about."

Jack Sigler laughed again. It was a good laugh. Warm even. Then Sigler looked down at Finkle's pack, and his smile widened.

"What, pray tell, is that?" Sigler pointed to the eight metal rods jutting out of the backpack.

"Ahem. Oh, that." Finkle could feel his face flushing. "Just some scientific accoutrements I've brought along for the expedition. I figure once we find the Fountain, we won't be able to bring it back with us, so I want to be able to study it before returning. The rods are part of an experiment I plan on trying once we get there."

Sigler shook his head, obviously amused at the answer. "That's so like you. Or at least, how I always imagined you to be."

Finkle thought of that for a moment, pondering just how much about himself the pirate actually knew. The man seemed to be almost intimately familiar with him, though he had no idea how. After a few minutes pondering this notion, an idea struck him. He cocked his head, then cleared his throat.

"What happened to you that last night on the ship, Captain Sigler?"

Sigler held up the compass, moving right to left, then clapped it on its side before looking over at Finkle. "What do you mean?"

"You've changed." He exhaled a plume of smoke and continued. "Three days ago, you were ambivalent toward our cause at best. Then the...er, attack came." Finkle shuddered at the memory of Sigler's bestial assault on the unsuspecting boarders. "Your attitude was decidedly different afterward. You seemed more committed. Clear headed. And if you'll forgive my saying so, infinitely more pleasant."

"Ah. That." He tucked the compass into his vest pocket and looked up into the tree canopy above him. The cries of strange birds and jungle fauna echoed through the trees, creating a sort of wild lullaby in preparation for the night. "It's simple really. As you know, I'm old, Mr. Finkle. Very old."

"I'm quite aware of that."

"Yes, but not aware of just how old I am. Try to remember something from your childhood. The best day of your young life before turning five years old. Where I'm from, it would be Christmas morning, but I know you celebrate the holiday differently than we do. So just think back to the happiest memory you have."

Finkle paused, closing his eyes. He pondered the question. His happiest memory. Bits and flashes sprang to mind, but sifting through each memory was troublesome. He could recall broad strokes of those memories, but the details were vague. Hazy.

"I remember the first time I was allowed to go hunting with my father."

"Good. Tell me about it."

"Well, I nearly shot a squirrel. Missed it ultimately, but I was damned close. I remember my father being so proud of..."

"What color was the squirrel?" Sigler interrupted.

"Pardon?"

"The color. Of the squirrel."

"Well, er, brown, I suppose."

"You suppose?"

"It was a long time ago. How can I remember something that trivial?"

"Let's make it something easier then. What color was your father's coat on this hunting trip?"

Finkle hesitated. "Uh, well, I believe..."

"It's fine that you can't remember," Sigler said. "That's my point. Now imagine that you're nearly three thousand years old. Three thousand years of memories that fade as time goes on. Imagine how that would make you feel. Imagine the pain of losing memories of the people most important to you. How would that make you feel, Mr. Finkle?"

He considered the question for a moment, and finally understood. Lanme Wa was old. Far older than he'd ever imagined. Three millennia. And no matter how fast the man healed or how fast or strong he might appear, he was still human. With a human mind. Though Finkle was not a biologist—had never studied the human brain as some of his contemporaries had—he'd read theories that there was a limit to the amount of information it could contain. After a while, some of the information would be expunged, so that new memories could take root. What would such a lifespan do to someone? How might it corrupt their soul? That invisible essence that made an individual who he was, based upon experiences. Could such a man as Lanme Wa be the same man he was when he was Jack Sigler?

"I think I begin to understand," Finkle said gravely. "What I don't get is why hide away in a casket? You're losing your memories of who you were. Why not focus on the man you are now and move on?"

"You've moved off topic." Sigler smiled and held up a finger, waving it reprovingly at Finkle like an old grandfather. "You asked what changed. You asked me why I was now so committed to this expedition."

"Oh. Yes. Right."

"The answer for the change was, quite simply, you."

"Me? How did I change your mind?"

Sigler's smile widened. "Our assailants noticed you. One of them pointed his weapon at you. He cocked the hammer back and was about to fire. That's when everything changed for me. When I realized something I'd never allowed myself to consider before."

"What's that?"

"Besides the loss of vital memories I've been experiencing over the past few centuries, there's something else that's been disappearing from my life as well." He picked a frond from a nearby palmetto bush and turned it over and over in his hand as he considered his next word. "Purpose."

"Purpose? How so?"

"It's long and complicated, and I'd rather not get into the details. But I'll say this: I spent the majority of my life fighting. Fighting for just causes. Fighting to protect people. Working to set right the travesties of history. Sometimes I would succeed. Other times, I failed miserably. Each time I succeeded though, nothing else changed. History moved forward just as it was meant to. After a while, I realized that nothing I did really mattered. No battle I fought changed the world one iota. So why bother? Why get involved? There've been a number of times I've hidden myself away from the world. Found a small farm in Italy, and tilled the land for grapes. Bought a fishing boat in Macedonia. Tried to live the quiet life. But every time, I'd be pulled right back into battles I couldn't do anything about.

"But then that sailor pointed his pistol at you, and I realized at that moment, the fallacy of what I thought to be true. If you were to be shot...to be killed...at that very moment, what would happen to the world I knew? I mean, you're one of the signers of the Declaration of Independence, after all! How would that affect history if you..."

"Wait! Stop." Finkle stood up. "How did you know about that?"

"Know about what?"

"We haven't told anyone about that. No one. We've met in secret about the possibility of officially declaring our independence from Britain. Up until now, we've just been pushing against unfair taxation. Against a great many maltreatments by King George. But a secret few have been considering completely breaking from Britain. But that's all it is...a discussion. It's one of the closest guarded secrets of the Colonies. So how do *you*—a man who's been in the grave the better part of a century—know about it?"

"What? The Declaration of Independence?" Sigler shrugged. "Like I told you, there's just some things I..."

"Captain!" someone in the camp shouted. "Captain!"

A few seconds later, Reardon appeared from his tent and ran over to an obviously terrified sailor. Finkle and Sigler moved over to the commotion to learn what had happened.

"She's gone, Captain." The sailor had bleeding gashes across his face, like the tips of hundreds of tiny claws had scored his cheeks. "The witch. I saw her trying to sneak away from camp. I followed her. Tried to stop her, but she...she did something to me. I don't know what. But she's gone."

18

"I would'na worry about it, Mr. Spratt," Reardon said to the bleeding sailor. "She was little more than dead weight to this expedition anyway. Good riddance, I say. She'll be dead before dawn in these sinister jungles."

"And I wouldn't be so sure of that, Captain," King said. "Asherah was raised in jungles far more dangerous than these. She's also a mambo bokor. No matter what you believe about vodou, Reardon, she does have some amazing tricks in that medicine bag of hers." He took the sailor gently by the arm. "Can you show me where you lost her?"

The man nodded as he dabbed the blood away from his face with a rag. "I think so, yes."

Without any more prompting, Spratt moved westward through the camp. King, Finkle and Reardon followed. Greer took up the rear, a long rifle clutched in both hands. When they came to the tributary, their guide made a right turn, and followed it north two hundred yards from camp. He then pointed to the water.

"She stripped bare, sir," the sailor said. "Then got in like she was goin' to bathe."

"And I suppose you decided to watch her, did ye?" Reardon asked.

The sailor's shoulders sank, and he gave a curt nod.

"Then what happened?" King asked.

"I still don't see why it matters," Reardon said. "She's gone. All the better, in my opinion."

King whirled around on him. "It's important because Asherah didn't agree to come here just to be my guardian or to wake me from my sleep. She had a reason for coming here, and trust me...anything that woman does should concern you greatly. We need to find out what she's up to, and fast." King turned back to Spratt. "What happened next?"

The sailor swept the hair from his downcast, nervous eyes. He winced as his palm brushed against the tiny lacerations covering his face. "Well, sir...um..."

"Answer him," Reardon growled.

"She, er, invited me to join her. I did'na think there'd be much harm in it, sir. She was smilin' at me. Pleased to see me, I thought." Spratt cleared his throat. "I took off me breeches and stepped in. That's when it happened."

"What? What happened?" Greer shoved the stricken sailor's shoulder, nearly bowling him over. "Tell us, man!"

King, still listening, had walked over to the water's edge and crouched down. One of the benefits of living for as long as he had was having a great deal of practice in hyper-observation, and what he'd seen at the river's bank was enough to elevate his normally steady heart rate. He picked up the object that had caught his eye and held it up.

"What's wrong, Captain Sigler?" Finkle asked, moving up next to him.

He turned the object over in his hand, and sucked in a breath. "A green army man." He said it out loud, but not to anyone in particular. "Plastic. Like when I was a kid."

He glanced up at Finkle. "I mean, a child. I used to play with these all the time. Collected whole armies of them. Had a set of Soviet soldiers, as well."

"What is...'plastic?'" Finkle asked.

King held up the figurine and the old man took it. "The material this is made of. Chemicals mixed together, then solidified to create easily malleable objects. But it won't be invented for another..."

"Are we concerned about some silly toy soldier or the witch, Mr. Sigler?" Reardon barked. "I'm still waiting to hear Mr. Spratt's answer to your question."

King looked over at the sailor, and nodded. "Tell us what happened after you entered the water."

Spratt gulped. "I ain't entirely sure. She held her arms out to me, beckonin' me closer. As I approached, somethin' grabbed me legs. Tendrils, like the tentacles of some raging squid. Lifted me straight up out of the water, it did. Then, vines exploded from the river and began raking me all over my face and torso. It was...it was..." The sailor suddenly collapsed onto the shoreline, curled up into a fetal ball, and his eyes went blank with terror.

"Poppycock," Greer said. "There are no squid in a fresh body of water, and vines don't have minds of their own. This man is simply trying to cover up his incompetence, at best. His treachery at worst."

King stood up, walked over to the trembling man, and placed a hand on his shoulder. Spratt looked up at him, and King tried to smile. Tried to reassure the sailor that everything was going to be fine. But at the moment, he wasn't so sure he was that good an actor. Despite Spratt's strange story of tentacles and vines—a story that King believed without reservation—he was more concern-ed over the presence of the plastic green figurine he'd found at the river bank. It was a minesweeper. The shaft that had once been the mine detecting device had long ago been chewed away, whether by some small child or by a pet. But even here, two hundred years in the past, the little toy was old.

"Captain Sigler?" Finkle was nearly whispering. "What should we do now?"

"Gather the men. We don't have time to rest for the night," King said. "We need to track Asherah down, before she accomplishes what she came here for."

"But what about the mission?"

"That *is* our mission, Mr. Finkle. You were right. I can't explain it, but this is definitely a place of immense power. Power that has inexplicably drawn the mambo bokor here. Whatever she's up to, it has to do with this place. With the Fountain." He turned to look at the expedition's three leaders. "I don't know what her plan is, but with her knowledge of vodou and the sheer power this place represents, it's the only thing that matters at the moment. Find Asherah, and we'll find your *Fountain of Youth*."

"Fine," Reardon said. "We'll do it your way. Let's get camp packed up and move on." He paused, and glanced back. "Mr. Spratt, come on, lad. Time we were a'movin'."

Spratt, however, didn't move.

"Spratt, I said get up and let's go."

Still, the sailor didn't move. King leaned to the side to get a closer look at him. He was still laying in a fetal position, his arms covering his face, but something appeared to now be covering him. Something green and spindly.

Finkle was the first to process what it was. "Dear Lord!" He dashed over and knelt down beside the man, jerking away strands of thorny vines that had wrapped themselves all around the man's body in the short amount of time they'd been talking. "Help me."

King was already moving before the request, his dagger drawn. He cut away a handful of the vines, then stopped. "Wait. Where are they coming from?"

"What do you mean?"

King reached underneath the sailor and pushed him forward so that his back was exposed. "The vines aren't coming up from the ground. So where are they coming from?" He rolled Spratt back the other way until his face was fully exposed. All four men gasped simultaneously. The tough, twine-like vines were growing quickly—in front of their eyes—sprouting from the many lacerations covering Spratt's face and chest. Three other tendrils swept out from the sailor's nostrils, and one larger vine twisted out from the man's opened mouth. He was already dead, King could tell that much. But what he couldn't quite fathom was what exactly had happened to him.

"Forget breaking down camp." King stood, and started running toward the camp. "We're out of time!"

19

Asherah ran through the tangle of vines and cypress, shooting quick furtive glances over her shoulder as she did. She couldn't be sure how long Lanme Wa and the crew of the *Reardon's Mark* would take to come after her, but she knew she needed to put as much distance between them as she could, if she hoped to succeed.

Of course, the vines attacking the hapless sailor had been a surprise. She'd hoped to lure the simpleton into the water with the promise of carnal sins, then cut his throat without anyone being the wiser. But the vines had a mind of their own. Had taken care of the problem without her having to bloody her hands. No doubt, it had been the work of a local l'wa, but until she became aware of the spirit's presence and personality, she could not be sure it would not turn its ire toward her, for bringing the white men into its realm.

So, with the thought of both Lanme Wa and the unknown l'wa nipping at her heels, she pressed on. For most of the voyage after the dread pirate's awakening, she'd remained sequestered. Not so much hidden as she'd tried to avoid any real interaction with any of the crew. There'd been no need to draw any unwanted attention to herself. But she'd been a constant presence, nonetheless. Always there around the corner, listening, watching. Gathering the information she would need to traverse the jungle alone, without the aid of any of the men. She'd eventually surmised the location of this so-called 'Fountain of Youth.' She knew she'd have to get there first, if she hoped to fulfill her promise to young William and cement her place as the most powerful of all mambo bokors.

Finding herself exhausted, she came to a halt and bent over, sucking in air slowly as she rested. She estimated that she'd traveled a good eight miles since breaking away from the camp. A good day's march in record time, by anyone's account. She needed to sleep, but she knew she didn't have the time. With her disappearance, Lanme Wa would not allow the others to rest. He'd come after her without thought of anything else.

His is such a distrustful mind, she mused with a wry smile.

The sound of wood cracking from nearby brought her to her full height, and she spun around to identify the sound. Another crunch. Something large and heavy lumbered somewhere off to her left. In the darkened woods, it was almost impossible to see one's hands in front of their faces, much less an unwieldy monster thumping around nearby.

She'd heard stories of the creatures that haunted the Florida swamps. Large reptiles—*alligators*—and giant snakes. Panthers the color of pitch. Great bears that could stand three heads above the tallest man. And that didn't even include the natives, who regularly hunted such creatures to survive. From what she'd heard from the sailors, nothing was more savage than the Indians that would slice the skullcap off one's head for a mere trophy.

But none of these things could possibly explain the immensity of the footfalls the beast near her made. Nothing so mundane could be that large.

A low, threatening growl echoed out from the darkness, followed immediately by a satisfied mewling. *A cat? No. That isn't the sound a cat makes. More like...*

She didn't finish the thought. She simply couldn't place the sound to any creature of which she was aware. She began turning three hundred and sixty degrees, squinting into the inky blackness around her. Then she saw it. A patch of blackness slightly darker than the rest of the landscape. A blackness that moved and swayed, less than fifty yards away from her. It stood over six feet tall and had a long pointed tail that hovered a few feet off the ground. Other than that, she could make out no more details. Wary, she clutched her medicine bag and prayed to whatever unknown l'wa protected this place. As powerful a sorceress as she was, she wasn't certain any of her magicks could safeguard her against such a nightmarish beast. So, she stood there, as still as possible, and she hoped the creature would pass her by.

Five minutes later, it had moved on, leaving Asherah breathless and unsettled. Though the local fauna was all so new to her, she would have expected to at least have some idea of what the beast had been. Instead, she was shaken with the realization that something so huge and monstrous lurked in this unexplored wilderness. Even more unsettling was the fact that the creature just felt out of place here. Something was not quite right about its presence. It was as if Nature itself had convulsed by the creature's invasion.

She shuddered at the thought, took a deep breath and starting making her way once more toward the

Fountain. This time, however, she decided to be a little more cautious as she walked.

The sun was edging up over the horizon; its rays were shining down through the trees and evaporating the dew covering the tree canopy above. A steamy fog began blanketing the jungle floor, obscuring King's vision as he pressed forward.

"How can we hope to find the witch in such a fog?" Captain Reardon asked. He, like everyone else in the expedition, had discarded his coat and rolled up the sleeves of his shirt. Yet he was still soaked to the bone with sweat and exhaustion.

"It's still early yet," King replied as he slid his sword back into his belt. He'd already picked up on her trail despite the poor visibility, and he no longer needed a blade to cut through the jungle growth. "It'll burn off soon enough. Right now though, she's leaving a trail big enough for a blind man to follow. She doesn't seem too concerned about concealing her path."

The humidity-fueled heat made breathing difficult. Each time he inhaled, he felt as though he was swallowing a gallon of warm water, and he knew the others would be having a much harder time of it than he. "Let's take a rest for a few minutes before moving on. No more than ten minutes. Enough to relieve ourselves, hydrate and ease our bare feet from our boots."

There was a collective sigh from the men as each of them found a nice spot to sit down and rest. King had to admit, this crew had impressed him a great deal. Despite the lack of a solid night's sleep for more than four days, they were still determined to move forward. There'd only been a few grumblers in the pack, and most of them had been the loudest in expressing their dismay over the unnatural way Spratt had met his end. They'd been the most superstitious of the lot, and they had protested moving further, lest they all succumb to the curse that plagued this land. They'd never really stopped their complaining since. Still, the vast majority of the sailors felt their mission was too important to the Cause. Too important to the Colonies' desire to show their British masters that they could, indeed, survive without them. In fact, in succeeding in their quest, they hoped to show King George that they could not only survive, but they would thrive.

They believed in what they were doing, and something long forgotten inside King began to stir at the thought. It had been so long since he had fought in a war in which he had been emotionally invested. So long since fighting for something in which he truly believed. And here he was, at the very birth of the nation he loved so dearly, and he had—up until now—been completely unmoved by it.

When did I become so callous? He took a swig from his water bladder as he gazed out into the morning jungle. *So cynical?*

His eyes caught something large, moving slowly through the trees nearly a hundred yards away. He looked around, but no one seemed to have noticed. When he glanced back, the large creature had stopped moving, and it had crouched lower to the ground. From this distance, with the foliage blocking a clear view, he couldn't quite make out what it was, but there was a sense of recognition there. Something about its posture. Its long, pointed tail that swept back and forth as it lumbered about. There was a name for it, but he couldn't quite remember what it was.

Something important. Something magnificent even.

It was also something that definitely did not belong here. In this place. At this time. The realization triggered the hairs on the back of King's neck to stand straight up.

"Finkle!" he half-whispered, half-yelled at the old man, as he was walking by. The scientist turned to him with a questioning look. "Come with me. Bring a musket, but don't let on about it."

"Why? What's going on?"

"Trust me, if this is what I think it is, you're definitely going to want to see it without the crew around."

Without another word, Finkle scurried back to where the men lounged, swiped a long-barreled musket, and returned to King. With a nod from the ancient pirate, the two melted further into the jungle without anyone noticing. They crept forward nearly fifty yards, coming to a clearing. Finkle nearly shouted when he saw the beast before them, but King clamped a hand over his mouth.

"Shhh. Just watch. We're in no danger as long as we stay perfectly still."

The two leaned forward, moving aside a cluster of palmetto fronds for a better look at the creature before them. Its head stood about seven feet off the ground, but its immense body could have easily measured thirty feet in length. It stooped over on its hind legs, with its forelegs nearly dragging the ground. Scales, salmon-like in color, covered its entire body, with a soft downy coat of pink and white feathers running down its back. Its large horse-like head reached up, plucking leaves from an oddly shaped bush, and its neck shook violently as it swallowed the vegetation down its long gullet.

"W-what is that?" Finkle whispered. His eyes were wide, but it didn't seem to be from fear. More like the look one gets from appraising priceless pieces of art in the Louvre. There was a sadness in those eyes, as well, which King couldn't quite understand.

"I'll admit something here. This is way over my head."

Finkle cocked his head, not understanding the figure of speech.

"What's happening here is *beyond my understanding*. If I remember correctly, dinosaur fossils won't be discovered for another fifty years or so." King pointed at the creature. "But that, my friend, will be called a dinosaur."

"*Terrible lizard,*" Finkle said, translating the Greek meaning of the word. "Seems appropriate...except for those feathers."

"That's a long story actually. But this particular type of dinosaur, if I'm not mistaken, is called an Iguanodon. They're herbivores. Harmless to us, and from all accounts, gentle."

"But you've seen all kinds of things," Finkle said. "I saw those bones in your graveyard. Why does such a creature as this perplex you the way it does?"

King watched as the iguanodon crunched down on a mouthful of leaves, before letting them slide down its long throat with another violent shake of the neck. "Dinosaurs have been extinct for millions of years. There shouldn't be any left."

"Oh." Finkle swallowed as he pondered the meaning of it all.

Of course, King knew there were tales of dinosaurs haunting the darkest recesses of the world even up until the twenty-first century. The Loch Ness Monster was one of the more famous. But the more he thought about it, the more he recalled something similar to what he was seeing now. A paper written by some whack-job crypto-zoologist named Jackson—or something like that—about a creature haunting the shores of the St. Johns River, known as Pinky. An iguanodon-like creature with pink skin that started making an appearance in the area in the late 1960s and on into the 1980s.

So is this it? Is this Pinky? King let those questions sink in. Could this living dinosaur still really exist in the modern world? With the discovery of the plastic army man the day before, King somehow doubted it. Two temporal anomalies in the same general vicinity, representing such extreme points in time...it just didn't seem like a coincidence.

"Finkle! Where the blazes are you?" Captain Reardon shouted from their temporary rest area. Suddenly, the dinosaur's head reared up nervously. Its huge nostrils flared back and forth with a powerful huff of air, then it bolted away faster than what seemed possible for its huge, unwieldy body. In less than three seconds, it had disappeared from sight into the forest.

"Blast that Irishman!" Finkle spat. "He has the uncanny ability to ruin even the most beautiful of things."

But King wasn't paying attention. Instead, he stood from his crouched hiding position, and was moving directly into the clearing. Toward the seven oddly shaped shrubs from which the dinosaur had been feeding. "Finkle, over here."

He heard the old scientist climbing out from the wooded blind they'd used to spy on the creature, but he didn't wait for the man. Instead, he brushed away a few of the stray leaves growing on a cluster of vibrantly green vines over the shrub. He let out a low whistle at what he saw.

Finkle came up next to him and came to an abrupt halt. "Is...is that what I think it is?"

King nodded. "Looks like our British friends beat us here," he said. "And suffered the same fate as Mr. Spratt."

20

Finkle stared at the macabre sight in front of him. Each of the seven shrubs had, at one time, been living, breathing human beings. From the tattered remains of what was left of their clothing, King was right. They had been British. Soldiers. God-fearing servants of King George. Now, they were like petrified, vegetative statues. More plant than anything else. Their skin had been ripped apart as tendrils of vines had encapsulated them, wrapping them in a living, photosensitive cocoon. Their extremities were almost wooden, still clutching their muskets with both branch-like hands. Their upper arms, torsos and heads were thick with vines, leaves and oddly colored flowers.

The flowers were more unsettling than anything, as the winter months were fast approaching. Even in Florida, plants didn't typically flower after the early part of May. So why were these poor unfortunate souls covered in them?

"Saints preserve us," Reardon said, as he approached the shrubs. "They're just like..."

"Spratt," Finkle answered. "We know."

"But how is it happening? What is causing this?"

King shrugged. "Not sure. But this is the third weird thing going on around here. Between the vines, the plastic figurine and the...er, creature we just saw, there is definitely something strange happening. And I have a feeling it's tied directly to this 'Fountain' you're looking for."

"Could it be the witch's doing?" Finkle asked.

"I don't think so. Don't think she's had enough time to set any of this in motion." King pointed down at the ground a few feet away from the shrubs. "But she's been here. There are her tracks. Looks like she's turned southwest."

"So what do we do now?" Finkle asked.

"Same thing we were already doing. We need to track Asherah and stop her. We just need to make one little alteration to the plan."

"What's that?" asked Reardon.

"Be mindful of the vegetation."

The three of them glanced around, taking in the thick walls of cypress and live oak, and the vast river cane breaks surrounding them. Their eyes scanned the thick, hanging strands of moss drooping from tree limbs, and the palmetto bushes blocking even the slightest trace of a path in every direction.

"That might be more difficult than it sounds," Finkle said, wiping a stream of sweat from his forehead.

"No kidding," King answered, before pulling his sword from its sheath, and slicing a path for the crew to follow.

Day 5

King struggled to breathe as he sat, cross-legged, in his bedding. No matter how much he struggled, he couldn't keep his hands from shaking at the memories flooding through his mind's eye. It had been nearly thirty minutes since he'd awakened, dripping in his own sweat. Still the experience had left him drained—despite his remarkable recuperative powers.

The day before, the expedition had finally broken away from the tributaries and come to the main body of the St. Johns River. Two more of the crew had succumbed to the strange vegetative transformation since they'd left the clearing with the human shrubbery, and one more man had been scratched and was currently under the watchful eye of the closest thing to a surgeon the crew had, the cook named Nichols.

They'd set up camp the night before and tried to rest, but the entire crew had been disturbed by grisly dreams from their pasts. Their worst moments, relived in vivid recollection, in a steady fit of REM sleep. King, apparently, had not been immune either. The faded memories of hundreds, if not thousands of souls, bleeding out as a result of his own sword, had played over and over in his dream state. The final image—the woman he loved, Sara, albeit an older one than he remembered, dying in his arms.

"O'Leary and Quinton won't wake up," Finkle said solemnly, from over King's shoulder. The old scientist looked as if he'd aged a decade overnight. Apparently, he too, had felt the brunt of a fitful night of terrors.

"What do you mean, they won't wake up?"

"Just as it sounds. They're breathing. Quinton's hair's gone snow white. Both their eyes are wide open, but they won't budge. They don't even blink. It's the damndest thing."

King looked up at Finkle. "Let me guess. Your night-mares—you were reliving the most brutal portions of your life. Right?"

"You, too?"

King nodded. "So that's the fourth oddity we've faced since entering this jungle," he said. "And the third having to do with Time."

"Beg your pardon?"

"Think about it. First was the army man figurine. That's from the future." King ignored the questioning glance Finkle gave him. "Then the dinosaur. From the past. Now, the dreams. Reliving moments from our past...and if I'm not mistaken, some scenes from our future as well."

"They were just dreams, Jack. Nothing more than that."

"Nightmares. From all accounts, every single one of us had them, except the few left as lookouts, and Nichols. But these weren't typical nightmares. There were no boogeymen in them. No monsters under the bed. There was no trying to run away, only to be caught in slow motion."

Finkle let out a half-hearted chuckle. "Your language continues to vex me so, my boy."

"My point is, these dreams weren't over-dramatized, surreal impressions of past events in our lives. If yours were like mine, they played out perfectly with history. There were no exaggerations. No metaphorical misrepresentations. They were perfect, play-by-play recollections of things that have happened to us in the past."

Finkle seemed to consider this for a moment before giving a brief nod. "I suppose you're right. But what does it mean?"

A blood-curdling scream erupted amid the shaken, weary sailors, interrupting King's and Finkle's conversation. A man leapt up from his bedding, facing to the north. His eyes were wild with terror.

"Da? It's not my fault," the sailor said. "I didn't mean to break it."

Finkle stepped forward, about to go to the man's aid, but King's strong hand stopped him. "Wait. Let's see what happens."

The sailor stepped back, raising one arm above his face. "Please, Da! I'm sorry!"

"Who's he talking..."

That was when they both saw it. A spectral figure ambled toward the disturbed sailor. Though near transparent, the figure was human shaped—a large, robust man with a cruel, angry face.

"Da, please, no!"

"W-what are we seeing here?" Finkle asked. "A ghost?"

"I don't think so. I think it's something else entirely."

Without warning, the transparent man raised a hand up and brought it down across the stricken sailor's face. The impact, loud enough to be heard from a hundred feet away, knocked the sailor to the ground.

"That's definitely no ghost!" King dashed forward, as the phantasm pressed in for another attack. It was about to strike the fallen man again, just as King's body slammed into it. A sudden arc of blue electricity ripped through the air where they met, sending a violent jolt through every muscle in King's body. Screaming, he fell to the ground, near the trembling sailor. King felt every single hair on his scalp, arms and legs stand on end as he sucked in a powerfully deep breath to force away the pain. When he looked up, the figure was gone.

"What, pray tell, was that?" Reardon asked, as he trotted up to King.

But King ignored him, and instead moved over to the still tearful sailor. "Are you all right?"

"I-I'm so sorry, Da! I didn't mean to drop your whiskey. It was an accident." The sailor's bloodshot eyes stared off past King's shoulder, as if the apparition was still as visible as it had been seconds before. A trail of tears washed away the dirt and grime covering the sailor's cheeks as he sobbed. The half-cleaned face now revealed a bright red and blue bruise, just below his left eye. Evidence of the blow he'd sustained. "The bottle just slipped outta my hand. I did'na mean for it to happen."

King looked around the campsite. Several—over half, if he wasn't mistaken—of the crew were packing up their things, and running into the jungle in the direction where they'd laid anchor.

"Wait!" Reardon shouted. "Come back here, ye cowards!"

But it was too late. One by one, the crew members disappeared into the vegetation carrying whatever they could. Now, only a handful remained, and most of them were wide-eyed—possibly paralyzed in place by fear.

"'Tis mutiny!" Reardon fumed. "Plain and simple. I'll see them hang if it's..."

"Captain!" King growled. "Calm down. Your man here needs to be tended to. We'll deal with your crew later."

Reardon nodded, then helped King lift the man from the ground. They dragged him over to one of the few remaining bed rolls left in camp. Carefully, they lowered him onto the makeshift bed, just as Nichols rushed over with a bucket of water and clean rag.

"I'll tend to him, Captain," he said, dipping the rag in the water and brushing it across the sailor's forehead.

A few minutes later, Reardon, Finkle, Greer and King huddled around the campfire, talking in hushed tones so that the remaining crew members couldn't hear what was being said.

"...so if that wasn't a ghost, what was it?" Finkle asked. The lines across his forehead were furrowed, and King couldn't tell if it was from frustration or from fear.

"All right. So far, we've experienced some pretty unusual activity since coming to Florida." King began counting off on his fingers. "First, there are the vines. We don't know what's causing them, but they seem to be infecting us somehow.

Turning us into...well, I'm not entirely sure. Second, we have the plastic figurine from my childhood."

"There's that toy again!" Quartermaster Greer spat. "Why do you keep bringing it up? Compared to what we've seen, that's the least of our troubles."

"If you'd let me finish, *Englishman*, I'll explain why it's so important." King glared at the quartermaster, causing Greer to shrink against his shoulders. "After the figurine, Finkle and I saw a creature that hasn't existed in millions of years." Greer opened his mouth to say something, but was instantly silenced by a warning glance from King. "And finally, this 'ghost' thing we all just witnessed. Only, I don't believe it was a ghost. As a matter of fact, when your man..."

"Jenkins. Robert Jenkins," Reardon said.

"When your man, Jenkins, gets himself under control, I'm betting we'll learn that the apparition was his father. Even more, I have a feeling Jenkins's father isn't even dead. I've got nothing substantial to prove that, mind you. Just a feeling."

"So you're saying he was attacked by the ghost of his father, who's still living?" Finkle asked. "How is that possible? A demon, maybe? Disguised as his father?"

King shook his head. "There have been at least four unexplained phenomena we've witnessed in the past few days. Of those four, one—the vines—is the odd man out. The other three have one common characteristic."

"And that is?"

"Time, gentlemen. The commonality is Time."

21

"How much farther do you think it is?" Reardon asked, glancing back at Finkle, who immediately riffled through the copied journal.

They'd left Nichols back at camp to tend to Jenkins and the young sailor who'd become infected with vine growth later that day. King had led them on their trek through the St. Johns River basin. Now, only eleven of the original twenty-three crew members in the expedition remained, and they marched warily behind King, Reardon and Finkle. Greer took up the rear, making sure no one else would decide to desert. They were following the river, bending back and forth from a southeast to easterly direction. The going would have been slow under normal circumstances, but as they took great pains to avoid contact with any of the surrounding vegetation, they crept along at an excruciating pace.

Finkle shook his head. "As I've said before, there aren't many landmarks written down. It's difficult to say."

"We're close," King said. He couldn't explain it. He didn't quite understand it himself, but he was beginning to feel an unmistakable tug toward their destination. Something deep within him had been guiding their trek for the past six hours. The closer they came to the Fountain, the stronger the feeling had become.

Whatever is going on, it has to do with Time Displacement, he thought. *Maybe since I'm already outside of my own time, it's affecting me differently than the others.* It was the only explanation he could come up with.

The entire situation had been beyond the understanding of Finkle's eighteenth-century mind. King had tried to explain his theory to them while back at the camp, but they couldn't quite grasp hold of what he was trying to say. Of course, it wasn't until the apparition of Jenkins's father had appeared that everything had clicked for King. The encounter had triggered a recollection of a theory he'd read once, about the possible true nature of ghosts. Something to do with folds in time occupying the same space simultaneously. The memory was faded. Difficult to pin down, but the gist was easy enough to grasp.

Time, the article had said, was not a straight line. It was more like a big ball of twine, clumped together. Certain points along the twine touched other points. When both points intersected with the material world, a *Time Fold* might be created, which would allow a person from one era to physically glimpse into the past or future. The theory speculated that when someone saw a ghost, they were actually looking into the intersection of two different points in time...seeing people or things of the past, slightly out of sync with the observer's own world.

That was the theory in a nutshell anyway, and it seemed to fit. Why it was happening here, in this jungle, King couldn't figure out. Nor could he grasp how the strange vine illness was part of it all.

But for now, that mystery would have to wait. At the moment, he was focused on Time itself and all it meant for the struggle he'd endured for nearly three millennia. Temporal waves crashing in from one time period to the other, were bringing the flotsam of another era into this one. The prospect energized him more than anything he could remember since being trapped in the past. If his theory was true, he might have just found a way to return to his own time without having to wait for the agonizingly slow ticking of the clock. He might be able to rejoin his family much sooner than he'd anticipated. That was, if he could get to the bottom of what was happening. And that simply required he continue assisting the aging scientist and the Irish privateer in their search for the mythical Fountain of Youth.

He'd done a lot crazier things for worse reasons.

"So have you seen any signs of the witch?" Reardon's question jerked King from his thoughts.

Honestly, King had almost forgotten about the mambo bokor, ever since forming his current theory of the strange phenomena. She'd simply ceased to be a priority for him, with visions of a way home dangling in front of his imagination. He chastised himself for such shortsightedness. It would be a grave mistake to become so blinded with the possibilities that he failed to see the knife in the dark.

King shook his head. "No, I haven't. We lost her tracks a while back." He hacked down a small sapling blocking their path with his sword. "But we can assume she's still heading for the Fountain. Maybe even already arrived, which means we need to be on our guard even more."

With the foliage blocking their way cut down, they started marching again. They walked several miles in silence, but King brought them to an abrupt halt when the jungle erupted with an ear-splitting screech from the other side of the river.

Brahaayaaaaaaah!

"What was that?" Reardon asked. "It didn't sound human."

"A bird, possibly?" Finkle offered.

Putting a finger to his lips, King motioned for silence. He crouched low, bringing his sword up in a defensive stance and keeping his eyes fixed on the opposite river bank.

"I say, what is going on up here?" Greer was barging toward the front of the line; his grating voice was an octave higher than normal. King spun around, slamming his palm over the quartermaster's mouth with a growl.

"Quiet," he hissed.

Another similar cry rang out from several miles away on their side of the river. It came from somewhere deep inside the forest.

"Whatever they are," King whispered, "there's more than one of them. And they seem to be communicating."

They huddled there, waiting for another ten minutes. When no more cries reciprocated, King stood up and glanced around. All was quiet. The only thing that could be heard was the ever-present chatter of birds and other Florida fauna foraging near the river.

"It seems as though whatever they were, they're not interested in us for the moment," Finkle said.

"I'm not so sure." King turned, scanning their surroundings. "Something just doesn't feel right."

"I say we move on," Greer stepped past King and brought up his musket to his shoulders. "Whatever it was will find quite a fight on its hands, should it choose to attack us."

King struggled against the urge to smack the irritating quartermaster across the back of his head. Then he noticed the fine red welt, hardly visible, across the back of the Englishman's neck.

"When did you get this?" King brushed the jagged red mark with his index finger.

"What? What are you talking about?"

"Oh, my." Finkle drew closer, pressing his spectacles up onto the bridge of his nose for a better look. "Is that a..."

"A scratch, yes." King placed both hands on Greer's shoulders, and spun the man to face him. "Try to remember. When did you get that scratch?"

Greer reached behind his head and felt for the scrape. His eyes ballooned out as he frantically began probing the mark with the tips of his fingers. "I-I wasn't even aware I was scratched. I've no idea when it happened."

"It's probably nothing to worry about," Captain Reardon said. His encouraging smile was anything but genuine. "Could've happened anywhere. Doesn't mean he's going to turn into some God-forsaken tree." He spat on the ground after he said it. "In a million years, I ne'er though I'd say a sentence such as that."

As if in answer, there was a shout behind them. Every man in the group turned toward the voice, guns, bayonets and swords at the ready.

"Captain!" The shouting was clearer now, as the shouter drew closer. And from the sound of it, the man was in a near panic. "Captain!"

A few minutes later, Rob Jenkins burst through the trees, turned at the water's edge and moved toward them at full speed. He nearly ran into one of his fellow crewmen before his legs gave out altogether, and he sank to the sandy bank. His eyes were bloodshot and wild. His mouth was twisted in a ghastly rictus of fear. His clothes were in tatters, revealing deep cuts to his chest, arms and legs.

Reardon crouched beside the man, taking him by both shoulders and giving him a steady shake. "Calm down, man! What's wrong?"

Jenkins trembled uncontrollably, gasping for breath between sobs. But King knew this fit was different from the one that had rendered him so inconsolable earlier that day. Before, the man's tearful sobbing had been from something more akin to guilt. Emotional pain, maybe. This was something else entirely. Something that could only be described as terror. One glimpse at the man's newly whitened streak of hair at his temples confirmed as much.

"It's Cook Nichols," Jenkins said, after struggling to collect himself. "He's dead. Ripped to pieces in front of me."

"What?" Reardon asked. "How?"

"It was Shawn O'Steen, sir."

King looked over at Finkle, a silent question on his brow.

"The young man who was infected by the vines. The one the cook was watching over in camp," the scientist whispered back.

Jenkins continued between labored breaths. "Something happened to him. He changed, just like all the rest. Nichols thought he was dead. We started packing up our gear, planning on rejoining you, when we heard the... the...most bone-chilling howl we ever did. When we looked in Shawn's direction, he was gettin' up from the ground. Only, it wasn't him. It was...it was somethin' straight from the pits o' Hell, I tell ye."

"Describe it." King stepped forward, his piercing eyes searching Jenkins's tattered body up and down.

"It looked different than the shrub-people we seen earlier. This was bigger. Much bigger. The vines wrapped around him were harder, full of thorns. The parts that were human you could see through the web of vines looked like they were covered in moss. The brightest green moss anyone's ever seen—even in Ireland."

"So it killed Nichols, but you managed to get away?" Greer sneered. He was baiting the scared man, and everyone knew it.

"Greer!" Reardon shouted. "Enough of that. Come over here and sit down, Jenkins." The captain led Jenkins over to a log, and helped him down. Then, he handed the man a filled water bladder, and smiled. "Rest here, while we discuss our options."

The captain turned to address the rest of the expedition just as the jungle around them exploded in a chorus of unearthly, bestial howls. Without further warning, the trees around them shook violently. The thunder of large footfalls echoed all around them, before three large plant creatures burst into view.

The group turned to run in the only direction they could—into the St. Johns River—but they were blocked by five more creatures wading up to shore and a wall of thick, thorny vines rising up from the water like monstrous tentacles.

"This can't be happening!" Greer shouted, taking aim at one of the creatures and firing. The metal ball slapped through the wood-armored chest of one of the creatures, ripping a hole through its back and disappearing into the woods beyond. The creature, however, appeared unperturbed by the impact. It rushed forward with another howl.

King lunged with his Grecian sword clutched in his hand. He wasn't entirely sure what was happening, but he knew enough to understand that this was a coordinated attack. It wasn't the mindless, instinctual act of unthinking monsters. It was precise. Well thought out. Organized. The creatures had trapped them, sealing off their only means of retreat, so that everyone could be picked off one by one.

As he approached the creature rushing toward John Greer, King brought the blade down on its extended, bark-covered arm with a bone-crushing smack. The sword sliced clean through, causing a spray of chlorophyll-green fluid to come rushing from the severed limb. The creature screamed while the arm began to regenerate. It then wheeled around, and backhanded King with its uninjured arm.

King flew backward and struck the ground with a thud. His vision began to darken from the impact, but he willed himself to stay conscious. Focused. When he looked up, the creature was lunging directly at him—its newly formed arm extended with dozens of sharp, thorn-like claws reaching for his torso.

22

As the creature's claws came within an inch of King's chest, the world suddenly grew dark. It wasn't the hazy blackness of unconsciousness that dimmed his vision, however. As he prepared to fend off the blow, he suddenly found himself completely alone in the woods. Where it had been near dusk just a second before, now it was deep into the night, just at the start of the twilight before dawn. The sky above swirled with hues of midnight blue and purple, trimmed at the horizon with a ribbon of pale blue. Stars flickered high above, with constellations completely alien to King.

Propped on his elbows, he glanced around. The river was much narrower now, little more than a creek really. The vegetation was denser. The air more tepid, almost suffocating.

Where am I?

Though the landscape was vastly different, his instincts told him he was precisely where he'd been when struck by the plant creature.

So what happened?

He knew the answer before it even fully formed in his mind. Somehow, like the plastic army man and the iguanodon, he'd slipped into Time. The question, of course, was when? The past or the future? Considering the size of the river and lack of erosion marks near the water's edge, he was guessing it was the past.

Deciding he needed a better look around, he tried picking himself off the ground, only to find himself pinned to the moist soil underneath him. He jerked his arms, struggling to propel himself up, but it was as if a five hundred pound weight was sitting atop his chest.

"Well, this is just great."

He tried again, but still, his body wouldn't so much as budge, other than to sink deeper into the wet, muddy soil. He lay there, struggling futilely to rise but failing every time. Minutes passed, and all he could do was keep constant vigil for any wild beasts that might be roaming the jungle. Eventually, boredom overtook him, and he decided to sleep, hoping his situation might improve under the light of day.

At sunrise, he awoke, but still was unable to move. Though he knew it was a ridiculous notion, it felt as if the Earth's gravity had quadrupled overnight. Then, there was also the dull, throbbing bite of pain welling inside his gut. He couldn't quite identify the source, but it was there all the same, and he didn't know why his body wasn't healing itself to remove the discomfort. After nearly eight more hours of increasingly intense pain, he fell asleep once more.

He awoke in the dead of night. An explosion, followed by a great rumble in the air had startled him from his sleep.

"Geez. What now?" He was beginning to think he would have been much better off sequestered in his sarcophagus on Kavo Zile.

He glanced up, homing in on the direction of the sound, just in time to see a blinding streak of red-orange light burning away the darkness. The falling object rumbled, the sound waves jarring King's bones from even this distance. It shot diagonally toward the ground. From its trajectory, he figured the object would strike the Earth three or four miles to the west, on the other side of what would become the St. Johns River.

The moment the calculation was completed, he was struck with another horrible realization. He was nearly at ground zero for a Volkswagen-sized meteorite that had broken through the atmosphere and was about to hit the planet. It was hardly a 'world-killer', but it would certainly play havoc on the general landscape for the next few millennia. And he wasn't entirely sure what its effects would be on even his incredible regenerative capabilities.

"Yep," he mumbled to himself, as he clenched his eyes shut and braced for the fiery tempest that was about to come. "I would have definitely been better off in my damned coffin." He inhaled deeply, then growled. "Well, shi—"

King returned to the future past in the blink of an eye, and he quickly discovered what had been causing the sharp pain in his abdomen. The plant-creature's spindly arm was pinning him to the ground with twelve-inch thorny talons. It had sliced him straight through the gut, exiting out his back. He screamed in agony, then opened his eyes to see the creature up close for the very first time. He stared into the monster's grisly face. Jenkins had been right. The creatures had once been human. Now, there was a complex webwork of hardened, bark-like vines covering every inch of their flesh in a mesh netting.

Their bodies were pocked with sharp, curved thorns. Looking past the thorns, where human flesh should have been, the body was stripped of skin and muscle tissue. The face, covered in a soft blanket of lush emerald green moss, was little more than a skull now. Dark recesses marked where the man's eyes had once been, completing the cadaverous appearance.

King wasn't sure whether the man had been one of Finkle's expedition or that of the British, but it didn't matter. He could see, however, that the human being that once was, no longer existed. He was dead. Which meant that King wouldn't have to pull any punches in this fight.

The thought brought a hungry grin to his face.

With a roar that matched the creatures', King's fist lashed out, pounding his attacker across the jaw. The flesh of his hand shredded against the thorny impact, but the force was enough to knock the monster aside. King watched as it tumbled over; its twelve-inch claws tore free from his torso. Blood gushed from the opened wound, but the injury healed rapidly, and King climbed to his feet.

With the brief moment he had, he gave a quick sweep of the landscape. The only men from the expedition still upright were Finkle, Reardon and Greer. But the quartermaster was on his knees, holding his stomach, as if in extreme agony. Finkle and Reardon stood back-to-back, swords outstretched and protecting their sickened comrade. King rushed over to them, scooping up his fallen sword along the way, and he turned his back to them as well, giving them a one-hundred-and-eighty-degree wall of protection for Greer.

The creatures lumbered toward them, not nearly as swiftly as before. King didn't know what was slowing them, but he wasn't going to look a gift-horse in the mouth. All around them, the remaining members of the crew—including Rob Jenkins—lay curled in fetal positions on the ground. The strange vines were working their way around the bodies, forming cocoons in which their transformations would occur. Eight creatures were bad enough. They needed to be long gone when the others emerged from their dormant states.

"Help Greer up," King said. Their backs were now to the river, and they were surrounded on all other sides. The vines still loomed behind them, but if King was right, he was already infected. He hoped his condition would help stave off the transformation, but for now, he was certain he could be quick enough to do what needed to be done. As long as his three living companions could follow through with their part.

One of the plant monsters suddenly lunged. King sidestepped, whirled around and brought his sword down across its overextended back. The creature wailed in pain, and stumbled to the ground. Before it could roll over, King was on top of it, hacking deep into its pulpy flesh.

"Run!" King cried. "Into the river."

The two men, Greer leaning on their shoulders, hesitated. They looked out at the tall, waving vines, then at King.

"I'm coming! Just go!"

This time, they obeyed. Kicking up their legs, they splashed through the shallow water as fast as they could. King gave one final swipe across the creature's neck, and then bolted after them. He passed them with little effort, swinging his sword as he ran and slicing through the tangle of malevolent vines. They reacted by whipping down upon him with a monstrous rage. Their thorns ripped and sliced at King, as he spun back and forth, cutting the vines at the base of their stalks and clearing a path through which Finkle and Reardon could carry

Greer. A minute later, they were on the other side of the wall, and swimming across the river. Fortunately, the current was weak, and they managed to stay on course, straight across. Not so fortunate, there were splashes behind them.

The creatures would be nipping at their heels in minutes.

23

The moment they reached the river's far side, King dashed around the embankment, collecting stray bundles of river cane, cattails and Spanish moss, carrying them as close to the shoreline as he could. Though it was dark, his companions could just make out the creatures heading in their direction.

"What are you doing?" Reardon asked, pointing toward the middle of the river. "They'll be here in seconds."

"Which is why we need to slow them down," King said. "Now help me. Gather as many flammable objects as you can, and pile them up along the shoreline."

Understanding dawning, the captain and Finkle laid Greer on the ground and followed King's instructions. Soon, they had a pile of debris about three feet high and ten feet across.

"Won't they just go around it?" Reardon asked.

King bent down in the center of the pile, and began striking a fine piece of flint he'd found against the blade of his sword. "I'm hoping they're not that intelligent," he said. "They're coordinated, sure. Organized. But they don't seem to have much in the way of free thought. I think they're little more than automatons controlled by a more intelligent mind."

"You mean the mambo bokor, don't you?" Finkle asked, adjusting his soaked pack across his back.

"Not sure yet."

A spark burst from the sword and stone. It flew into the debris, started smoking, then died out. King glanced over the wall. The creatures were now only about twenty-five yards away. He struck the blade again and again, until triggering another spark. This time, it landed in a pile of dry moss and began to glow. Carefully, King blew into it, until a single flame flickered to life and began licking at other pieces of debris. Soon, the entire structure was on fire, and his two companions whooped a cheer of excitement.

"Okay. We need to get out of here," King said, standing up and turning to face his companions. "This will only delay them. Not stop..."

His voice trailed off as he gazed past Finkle's shoulder. Finkle and Reardon turned, following the direction of King's gaze, and they both took in a deep breath. Greer lay on the ground, entirely encased in vines.

A moment later, King pointed toward the forest's edge. "This way. The Fountain is this way!"

They didn't question him. Instead, they all gave one last glance at John Greer's plant-encased body, then dashed into the jungle.

24

They ran for nearly two miles, making brief stops along the way so that Finkle could catch his breath. When King decided they'd put enough distance between themselves and the creatures, he allowed their pace to relax, and they began hiking at a much slower pace.

"You're bleeding," Finkle said. He was filthy. Covered in sweat, algae and grime, and his gait now came with a distinct right limp as he tried to keep pace.

King nodded at the observation, but kept his eyes fixed dead ahead.

"Will you change into one of those...those things?"

"I don't know."

He sliced through a patch of briar, clearing a path for them. From the little bit of the sky that was visible above the tree canopy, it was approaching midnight. The air was thick with swarms of mosquitoes that nipped freely over their exposed skin. King allowed himself a slight smile. The blood-gorging insects were some of the few mundane things they'd experienced since arriving in Florida, and he was grateful for them.

"Those things are near indestructible, laddie," Reardon said behind them. He kept looking over his shoulder, expecting a vegetative ambush at any moment. "Wonder what a bloke like ye'd be, if ye turned into one of them. I shudder to think of it."

King ignored the comment. He needed to think, and conversation at this point was only a distraction. He'd either turn, or he wouldn't. There was no point in worrying about it now. At the moment, his mind was working over another problem. Two of them, in fact.

First, was the issue of the creatures themselves and how they fit into this whole debacle. What did they have to do with the Time Folds? What did the Time Folds have to do with the Fountain of Youth? He was beginning to grasp the answer to the second question, but the first eluded him.

The second issue he needed to work out occurred to him while trapped in the past, earlier that evening. While lying there on the ground, listening to the gentle trickle of the ancient creek, he had thought about Rob Jenkins and his father. How his father had appeared to all of them...a ghost from the past. But there was one major problem. The Time Fold theory only worked with Time, not space. It occurred when two objects from different time periods occupied the same space. It wouldn't transport matter from one Place/Time to another. King doubted that the senior Jenkins had ever stepped foot on the Florida peninsula, much less into the teeming jungle of the river basin.

So how did he appear? How could he have possibly been here?

Did it really even matter? He wasn't sure, at this point, that anything mattered. For the first time in his very long life, he saw no way out. Sure, he wasn't really worried for his own life. He'd survived a great many strange and terrible things since being tricked into drinking the elixir that had made him near-immortal. This shouldn't have been any different. It was Finkle he was most concerned about. Finkle *had* to survive. For the future of the nation. For what America was to become.

As he glanced over at the old man's stooped form, his face downcast and understandably afraid, King found it difficult to be optimistic for the man's chances.

"Do I see a light up ahead or are my aged eyes playing tricks on me?" Finkle asked. His voice was weak. Hoarse.

King brought them to a sudden halt as he scanned ahead. Sure enough, there was the faint flicker of light dancing in what appeared to be a clearing, about a quarter of a mile ahead. His heart began to race. A campfire. Was it the British? Asherah? Or someone else? Perhaps the Native Americans that still called this land theirs. None of these options were particularly reassuring.

"Stay here. Rest," he whispered to them. "I'm going to take a look."

He handed Reardon his sword. Their powder was still wet from the swim across the river, and the captain had lost his sword in the fight. King refused to leave the two of them there defenseless, but he would be able to move much quicker and more silently on his own. Reardon accepted the sword with a grateful nod, and King crept away toward the light.

He snuck through the bramble and vines, unconcerned any longer about infection. He came to the perimeter of an open marsh. Algae-infested scum blanketed the stagnant water being fed from underground springs. From its filth, King guessed the marsh had no outlet.

A massive live oak, sixteen feet in diameter, sat in the middle of the marsh. Its roots, stretching for more than a hundred feet in every direction, jutted up from the water in several places. Its limbs, almost as long as its roots, branched out like the legs of an enormous upside down spider. Their own weight, however, was such a burden that they hung low to the ground.

The entire tree—something of wondrous beauty to King—was covered in a thin film of velvety moss, which was accented by more of the familiar Spanish variety hanging like tinsel from a Christmas tree. The entire thing looked as though elves should reside inside it, making cookies. There was something utterly magical about it, which set King's nerves on edge.

He glanced down at the base of the tree, where a large obsidian-like boulder sat in the mud. The oak appeared to have grown up around the stone, wrapping its trunk around it, like a child hugging a rubber ball.

Pulling his eyes away from the oak, he surveyed the rest of the marsh. On the northwest bank, there was a small campfire burning. Though it was the only sign of recent human activity, no one seemed to be tending the fire now.

He held his breath, focusing his hearing on the slightest trace of movement. Telltale signs of a trap. But there was nothing.

He looked back toward Finkle and Reardon, but the darkness and thick woodland obscured them from view. *As long as they stay where they are, they should be fine*, he thought. *Which gives me the luxury of throwing caution to the wind.*

King was just preparing to step out into the clearing when a feminine voice spoke. "Welcome, Lanme Wa. You are most welcome."

The voice was distinctly Asherah's, but something was wrong. It sounded different somehow. Muffled and amplified at the same time. Still, he was getting no closer to the answers he sought by crouching where he was. And the mambo bokor obviously knew he was there.

He stepped out from his hiding place, and into the knee-high water of the marsh. His boots sank deeply into the muddy bottom, as if it was working desperately to suck him down into the bowels of the Earth.

"Asherah!" King glanced around, wrinkling his nose at the fetid waters. If this was the 'Fountain of Youth,' it certainly wasn't living up to the hype. "Show yourself!"

"Not just yet, *monsieur*. First, we talk. Then, we see what happens, no?"

"Fine. Talk to me, witch."

She let out a soft tinkle of laughter, then mewled like a satisfied kitten.

"Oh, we have much to discuss, O' Man Who Never Dies. Great King of the Sea."

King tried to focus on where her voice was coming from, but was unable. It was as if she was everywhere at once.

"For years, I was terrified of you, *mon cher*. Fearful of da power you yielded. It is why I continued serving you, even after da death of my grandmamma. Da l'wa of Kavo Zile were weak. I knew dey could never protect me from you, should da day ever come. But things are different here in da New World! Things are better with Papa Guillaume at my side."

King stepped closer to the tree. His hands curled into white-knuckled fists, ready for whatever the witch threw at him.

"Papa Guillaume?"

"William." Finkle's voice startled King. He spun in its direction to see both the old man and Reardon standing at the edge of the marsh. Three of the plant creatures stood behind them, blocking their retreat. A fourth stood off to their left. Its shoulders sagged, and King could tell its flesh had yet to be removed. Somehow, he knew he was looking at what was left of Quartermaster Greer. "The slave," Finkle continued. "The slave that you killed on Kavo Zile. That's Papa Guillaume, isn't it?"

Asherah laughed again. "You silly boy! You know I didn't kill da man. It was da Brave Ghede did dat...most pow'rful of da l'wa on my islands. A payment for da honor of waking da doomed Lanme Wa."

Something unseen plopped in the water in front of King, triggering ripples that extended out toward him with ominous intent. A moment later, a human head rose up from the murky marsh, followed by a slender neck, shoulders and bare, round breasts. King gasped at the sight.

A network of vines clung to her flesh like long, wooden leeches. They spiraled down her arms and legs, around her torso and behind her neck, where the tip impaled itself into the back of her skull. Unlike with the other plant creatures, her skin had been left intact, though her face was drawn up, as if she hadn't eaten in months.

"Asherah, what have you done?" King asked.

"Oh, dis? Ain't not'ing. Dis is just me in da embrace of Papa Guillaume. He strengthens me, and now, I am very much like you, Lanme Wa. In his arms, I can't be killed. My heart will beat forever, and I'll be da most powerful mambo bokor who ever lived." She giggled. "And you, brave Capitaine, will be my servant forever."

An intense stab of pain shot through King's gut. His muscles spasmed violently, sending him to his knees. He clutched wildly at his stomach, as he screamed in agony. He felt something inside him, growing—tearing at his insides to escape.

"Now you see," Asherah said, walking up to King, and placing a gentle hand on his shoulder. "Papa Guillaume is da forbearer of a whole new tribe of l'wa. You got da seed of Papa Guillaume inside you, and soon, you will be his Baron and *my* consort."

King ripped the front of his shirt open and looked down. Something large, and snakelike writhed inside his gut, until muscle and skin tissue began to rip apart. He watched as a thorny, green tendril slithered out from the opening, and began wrapping itself around his body, starting to form a cocoon. His arms still free, he reached for it, trying to rip it out from his insides, but the roots were far too strong. Soon, the vines coiled around his arms, locking them in place and immobilizing him, working their transformative magic.

25

"Stop it!" Finkle shouted. "You're killing him!"

Asherah glared at the old man. "We've killed lots of men today, *mon cher*. What's one...no, three more?"

She moved toward them with effortless grace. Where the mud and muck worked to suck them down, Asherah seemed to skim the water like some humanoid dragonfly. When she reached them, she stepped toward Finkle and stroked the stubble of his chin.

"I have to admit though," she said. "You are a fascinating man. Unlike any of da men from dis one's crew." She nodded at Reardon, as she said it. "You were never afraid of me, and for da most part, you treated me kindly. I want you to know, I appreciate dat."

"If I knew what you would become, I might have acted very differently toward you, young lady."

She laughed at that. "No, you wouldn't. You don't got it in you to be rude to a woman."

Finkle glanced over at Jack Sigler, writhing in chest-deep water, as the tendrils continued to encase him. Unlike with the others, the vines hadn't come out of his body's orifices, but instead had exploded from his chest. Finkle wasn't sure why, but he hoped it had something to do with the man's amazing physiology. He could only hope that Mr. Sigler could find a way to beat the infection, and it was up to Finkle to buy the man more time.

"So tell me, you said this new loa of yours is William. How did you manage that?"

Smiling provocatively, she leaned forward and whispered in his ear. "It was my promise to him, *mon cher*. If he sacrificed himself to da Brave Ghede, I would make him greater dan anyt'ing he could ever imagine." She kissed Finkle's cheek and took a step back. "I collected his blood and brought it to dese dead waters. Poured da blood after da proper incantations back on da ship, and young William's spirit took hold. T'was da most amazing thing I ever did see, too. He took to l'wa life like a dove to da air, and within minutes, he was da most powerful l'wa ever to exist, with a reach far and wide within dis New World."

"I...I...can tell you...grrrrr...why," Sigler said between gasps.

Asherah whirled around. "What could you possibly know, dat I don't?"

Despite the obvious agony he was enduring, the pirate laughed. "I know what this place is. How it works." He broke down in a fit of coughs before he could continue. "The Spanish...they didn't mistranslate, as I had thought." Blood began trickling from Sigler's nose and mouth as he gritted his teeth in another spasm. "It's just that the Caribe Indians didn't have a word for this. They...they had to use a word closest to what they were experiencing, only it wasn't the 'Fountain of Youth'. It was probably something more akin to the 'Fountain of Life'."

Though wracked with pain, the fact that Sigler was talking brought a well of hope springing up in Finkle's chest. Hope that the man's body was expelling the strange infection and that he would soon be free.

"Time." Sigler jerked into a sudden convulsion, grasping his abdomen fiercely from another attack. "The Caribe Indians had no concept of time, not like we do. But they... they understood. Understood that this place can transport someone backward and forward in time. Make one experience life as...as a child again. Or show them a glimpse of what's to come."

Asherah's eyebrows arched. "What does dis have to do with Papa Guillaume?"

"Simple. Point of origin to the temporal..." More coughs. "Temporal anomalies, is that tree. More specifically, that hunk of rock it grew around. I saw it fall to the Earth. Thousands of years ago. It's a meteor. Probably emitting some type of radiation and..."

"Radiation?"

"Invisible. Energy. Somehow, its radiation is...is tangling up Time. Messing with it somehow. When you dropped William's blood in that marsh, he was instantly and simultaneously at the beginning of time and at the end. However much of Time is wrapped up in this tangle, that's how long his consciousness has been around. Millions of years to grow stronger and stronger."

Asherah's eyes sparkled at the news, and she twirled around in the water in joyful adulation. "Dis is even better dan I ever imagined. Not just an immortal l'wa, but an eternal one."

A splash pulled Finkle's attention away from the mambo bokor and back over to where Jack Sigler had been only moments before. Now, there was only a ripple, where he'd apparently collapsed into the marsh.

"Captain Sigler!" Finkle shouted.

Asherah turned to where Sigler had been and suddenly grew pale. After a moment, he exploded from the water, gasping for air. Finkle's hope instantly deflated, however, when he noticed the man still tangled by the web of vegetation. After a few minutes, expelling water from his lungs with deep, hacking coughs, he looked back over at the bokor.

"Look, I'm not certain if that's your William...or not." Sigler whipped his head around to clear his long hair from his vision. A stream of blood poured from his nose, but somehow, it didn't look as bad as it had before. In fact, there was hardly any sign of pain in the pirate's face. "Chances are, you just poured someone's dead blood into this cesspool, and something else entirely has been pulling everyone's strings. A parasite in the meteor, perhaps. Who knows? I've seen a lot of weird shit in my time on Earth. But there's one thing you need to be asking yourself right now, Asherah. Something important."

"And what is dat, Baron Wa?"

Sigler turned to look Finkle dead in the eyes. There was a hidden meaning behind the gaze, but the old man couldn't discern what it was. Sigler then turned back to Asherah.

"Why does Papa Guillaume even *need* you?" With effort, Sigler stood to his feet. The vines lashed around his body visibly tightened in response, but still the pirate stood defiantly. "It has the power to take over anyone it comes into contact with. It has all the servants it could ever need." The tangle around his legs snapped, and he took a step closer to the witch. Finkle nearly laughed when he saw her wince backward in fear. "Whatever this thing is, I think it's empathic. Has the ability to know our greatest fears or deepest longings. That's how Jenkins's father materialized in front of us. He was never here. Not in this place, but Papa Guillaume used the man's fears against him. Took matter from the time stream and created a remarkable facsimile to heighten Jenkins's fears, making him more susceptible to mistakes, and easier to take, when the vines came. It did that to all of us, to some extent. So with power like that, why in the world would it need you to retain your own autonomy?"

"Because he...he..." Her brows furrowed. "You're trying to confuse me!"

"Not at all." Sigler took another step forward. His arms and shoulders struggled against the bindings, and two more snapped free. "I'm trying to open your eyes to the danger you're in. As a matter of fact, with its roots inside you, it might already be too late." He gestured toward the remains of John Greer. "Like the quartermaster over there."

"Dat pig had it comin'. Da way he treated poor William in da boneyard. But I saved him! I protected him! I made him better dan before."

Sigler shrugged. "If that even *is* William. That's a big 'if.'"

Asherah shifted her gaze from Sigler to the ancient oak, as she bit at her lower lip.

"I know it's him. He talks to me."

Another snapped vine. The pirate was nearly free of his bonds, but Finkle was suddenly uncertain how that would help. As he looked around the marsh, he began to see dozens of the plant creatures lurking in the shadowy confines of the jungle. Though they stood there like statues, Finkle could feel their eyeless orbs taking in everything that was transpiring. At any minute, they could be mobilized and rip everyone to shreds. Lanme Wa was amazing, but even he couldn't overcome a mob of these monsters.

"Then I say it's time he levels with you," Sigler said to the woman. "Ask him to show you your future. See for yourself."

Asherah hesitated, then turned to face the oak.

"Papa Guillaume. Da Baron blasphemes you. Show him his words are untrue." She raised up her arms pleadingly. "Reveal to me what is in store for your servant!"

A thorn-tipped vine shot up from the water and slammed into the back of Asherah's neck. She attempted to scream, but she was silenced before the air could escape her lips. Her arms fell slack, and she fell unconscious right where she stood.

The moment she did, Jack Sigler snapped the remainder of the bonds, and he rushed over to Finkle and Reardon.

"Are you injured? Any scratches when they caught you?" he asked.

Finkle checked his arms, legs and neck, then shook his head. "I don't think so. What about you, Captain?" He turned to look at Reardon, whose eyes stared blankly, straight ahead. "Reardon?"

Finkle had thought the Irishman to be uncharacteristically silent, but he had assumed the man had simply been processing the strangeness of all that had transpired. He knew better the moment he laid eyes on the tiny vegetative web crisscrossing up Reardon's neck.

"They've got him."

Sigler nodded. "I noticed the moment I saw you two." He paused. "I'm sorry. But I don't know how much time we have, Mr. Franklin. I'm going to need those lightning rods in your pack."

26

Benjamin Franklin started at the use of his real name. He'd not heard anyone mutter it since leaving France, in search of a privateer for this expedition. General Washington had believed that Franklin's notoriety would have been more of a hindrance to their mission than anything else. And if the British caught wind that the scientist was leading the hunt for the Fountain of Youth, he would have been an instant target.

So, using his own proclivity for pseudonyms, he'd dreamed up 'Jim Brannan Finkle.' An anagram of 'Benjamin Franklin.' Of all the people who could have figured it out, Jack Sigler was the last one he'd have suspected.

"Um, but why? Why do you need my rods?"

"Because we're going to make a little lightning." Sigler grinned as he turned him around with a shove of his hands, and wrenched the eight rods from the backpack. "Now stay still. Those creatures won't come after you as long as—geez, I can't believe I'm actually going to utter these words—as long as the tree thinks you're playing by the rules." Sigler turned suddenly solemn, and drew the sword from Reardon's belt. "This is all about you now, Mr. Franklin. No matter what happens, I've got to keep you safe."

With that, King clutched the rods to his chest with one hand, gripped his sword with the other and began running toward the great oak tree. Seeing his sudden rush, one of the creatures bolted from its spot and charged straight at him. Without stopping, King ducked underneath the creature's outstretched arms, and jammed one of the lightning rods through its torso. It screamed pitifully as it struggled to pull the iron rod from its chest, giving King time to move past it, bound up the tree trunk and take hold of its nearest limb.

Once secure, he pulled himself up and began climbing hand over foot until he reached the very center of the tree's trunk. King felt it odd that a creature capable of controlling the movement of vines—organisms with no muscular system—didn't seem able to manipulate its own limbs.

The marsh filled with the howls of dozens of creatures as they began scrambling through the water to intercept him. He now had his answer. Why bother moving something as enormous as the oak, when it could get others to do all the work?

Not waiting to see if the human trees could, in fact, climb trees, he set to work on his plan. Sheathing his sword, he laid six of the remaining rods down on the limb, gripped the seventh in both hands and brought it down into the trunk of the tree. The oak shook violently with the impact, followed immediately by agonized wails from the plant creatures below.

Huh. Interesting.

Satisfied that the rod was securely impaled into the wood, he grabbed the other rods and scrambled up one of the larger limbs. Once he reached a thick heap of Spanish moss, he wrapped another of the rods within the tangled mess, and moved toward yet another limb. He continued this routine three more times, until he returned once more to the center.

The creatures now surrounded the base of the tree, their branch-like arms stretched up to the sky. The one he'd impaled with a rod stood closest to the base, the metal shaft still protruding through its torso. Slowly, each of their limbs began growing, inching closer to him with every passing minute.

"There's not a cloud in the sky!" Franklin shouted from the other side of the marsh. "What good are those lightning rods going to do?"

King ignored the comment, and glanced down at the creatures. Their clawed limbs continued to grow, inching closer to where he stood. He then looked over to where Asherah still stood in her trancelike state—a state, King guessed, similar to what he'd experienced when he'd been transported into the past to see the meteor crash. During that ordeal, he'd subconsciously been aware of what had been happening in the present. He'd felt the sting of the creature's claws in his gut. He'd been unable to move from his position because he'd been pinned to the ground in his own time. He only hoped the same would be true with the mambo bokor.

Okay. Now for the tricky part.

King leapt from his perch, brandishing the two remaining rods in both hands. Crashing down on three of the nearest creatures, he rolled and came up in full swing. The lightning rod in his left hand slammed into the chest of the first creature he saw. The one in his right hand followed suit into the next creature. Then, he ran at full speed toward Asherah, grabbed her by the neck and twisted her around to face the oak.

"Stop!" he shouted, drawing his sword with his free hand, and bringing it up to the woman's neck. The creatures instantly obeyed, freezing in their tracks. "I don't know what you've got planned for Asherah, but I'm betting it's important."

There was a murmur, like the sound of leaves blowing on the wind, coming from the army in front of him.

"I know you don't care for her, but I'm betting my life you *need* her for something."

More murmuring.

"Look, I don't want to destroy you." King glanced back at Ben Franklin. "You're my answer. My only hope. I need to get back home before I lose myself completely. But I must protect that man over there. I have to ensure his survival."

In unison, the creatures all turned to stare at the Founding Father, and the indecipherable murmuring grew in intensity.

"Let us go. Let us leave in peace. If you'll allow me, I'll return here to request your help in getting back to my own time." He eased up on Asherah's throat, and took a single step back. "What do you say?"

In response, dozens of tentacle-like vines stretched out of the water, and slowly whipped their way to encircle King, preventing any retreat.

"Don't. Don't do this!"

The creatures turned their hollow gazes on King once more, and began closing off any gaps in the barricade. Then Asherah's eyes snapped open. The thorny vine lodged in her neck slipped away, and she spun around to sneer at King. "Papa Guillaume's got no interest in making deals wit' you. You worth more to him as his Baron dan you are back in your own time."

"And you? Did you see what your precious loa has in store for you?"

She hesitated. "He don't need to show me not'ing. I be his queen. I know dat much."

"Let me guess...you saw nothing but darkness, didn't you?"

"I...I..." She turned back around to face the ancient tree. "I don't remember... I..."

Suddenly, the vines around Asherah's body sprang to life, encircling her exposed skin until she was fully cocooned in a husk of vegetation.

"Dammit!"

King grabbed his sword with both hands, and then crouched in a defensive position. "Mr. Franklin, when I say 'run,' you need to move like there's no tomorrow. Got it?"

"But I can't leave you... I have to stay and..."

"You need to escape. What I'm about to do is going to be too dangerous for you to be anywhere near."

A second passed, then the old man nodded. "Fine. I'll do as you ask."

King smiled at this, then turned back toward the tree. For the first time in centuries, the immortal pirate spoke a silent prayer, then prepared himself for a pain he'd hoped never to endure. He recalled his dream from the night before. Visions of his past and glimpses of his future. He mentally rifled through each image until he found the one he sought.

The emotional impact sent him to his knees. In his mind's eye, he saw Sara, dead in his arms. A trail of blood ebbed from the corners of her stricken lips. Her eyes stared blankly off into space, past his shoulder. He had no idea how she'd died, only that she was no more, and it cut a swath of agony into his very heart.

The leaves of the oak shuddered in sync with King's silent anguish. He'd been right. Whatever inhabited the tree was empathic. It felt. And it used those feelings to lash out physically at those it would attack.

And as King had predicted, the unthinkable materialized in front of him. Sara stood, just two feet in front of him. Angry, hate-filled eyes burned down at him, as she crossed her arms over her chest and spat.

"You should have saved me!" she raged. "You should have been there to protect me! Only, you weren't. You had other priorities. Other missions to take you away from me."

Tears streamed down King's cheeks as he looked up at her. His gut curled into a million knots with each accusation.

"I'm sorry. I'm so, so sorry." He wiped the tears from his eyes. "I tried. I tried to be there, but I just couldn't."

"Look at me, Jack!" She pointed down, next to his feet. He followed her gaze to see another Sara, dead in the water. The way she floated there seemed obscene. Her limbs bobbed up and down in a ghastly imitation of a marionette. "You should have saved me!"

"Run, Franklin! Now!" he screamed. Then he lunged. Salt-stinging tears clouded his vision as he leapt, but he extended his sword arm, and pierced the apparition's gut with the blade. The moment both bodies slammed into each other, an explosion of red-glowing electricity blossomed out into the marsh. Tendrils of lightning branched out, striking the creature with a rod in its stomach, then the next, until it arced up toward the first lightning rod embedded in the tree's trunk.

The energy shot through King's own system, sending his muscles into intense spasms. But he managed to keep focused, as the electricity shot out toward the rods throughout the entire tree, igniting the leaves and moss as it struck. Within seconds, the entire thing was engulfed in flames. The plant creatures dropped into the water, writhing in agony.

King leapt to his feet and glanced around, but Sara was no longer there. There was also no sign of Asherah's cocoon, but he had no time to puzzle over its disappearance. Instead, he bolted from the marsh, and ran in search of Benjamin Franklin.

EPILOGUE

King stood on the quarterdeck of the *Reardon's Mark*, carefully navigating the ship into the deeper waters of the Atlantic. The plan was to sail out toward the islands, then turn north, to make for Philadelphia as quickly as they could. The trick would be avoiding any British patrols still scouring the water in search of their missing expedition, but King thought he was up to the challenge.

He glanced out off the port side and saw the *Presley's Hound* keeping pace. He knew the watchful eyes of his own crew would keep them safe from almost any assault they might encounter.

"The crew's a bit shaken, but I think most are excited to start the journey home," Franklin said, as he ambled up the steps to the quarterdeck. "Only twelve of them remain, but that should be more than enough to sail this little cutter."

King nodded, keeping his hands fixed to the wheel.

"Listen, I know what you gave up for me back there," Franklin said, biting down on his pipe and lighting it. "It was a way home, wasn't it?"

"It could have been. But whatever that thing was, it had no intention of allowing me to use it."

"About that...do you think it really was that poor slave? William?"

"I honestly have no idea. I never really believed in magic when I was younger, but I've seen things in my time that have made me rethink my position," King said. "It could have just as easily been a natural phenomenon of some kind. You probably don't know this, but there are actually types of fungi that attach themselves to insects and control their actions. Lead them to water so they can thrive, even at the expense of the insect's life. So who knows what was inhabiting that tree?"

They continued in silence for nearly half an hour, watching a pod of dolphins playing on each side of the ship. Finally, Franklin spoke up.

"So what will you do now? Once you've safely delivered me to General Washington?"

King winced at the question. He wasn't sure. His soul still felt ripped apart by the image of Sara dead in his arms and by the haunting accusations she'd hurled at him. He didn't know how far into the future he'd seen. Wasn't certain when in her life she would eventually die, but one thing was clear...when he was finally with her again, he'd do whatever it took to become mortal again. To grow old along with her. And hopefully, he'd be there with her when that final moment came. But for now, he'd have to live with that memory, and he wondered if he wouldn't be better off returning to Kavo Zile to hide from the world once more, until it was time to see Sara and Fiona again.

"I honestly don't know," King said, realizing it had taken him far too long to answer if he wanted to avoid a potential pep talk from the great Ben Franklin.

Fortunately, the old man was far wiser than King gave him credit for. Instead of the anticipated lecture, Franklin merely nodded, then said, "Well, if you're interested, I believe we might have some work for you in the coming days. We could definitely use a man of your...ahem...talents."

King smiled, then gave him a nod. It was still a long journey to reach Philadelphia safely. Plenty of time to consider his next move. But he had to admit, a chance to experience the events that would ultimately lead to the formation of the greatest nation on Earth was a temptation he found himself struggling to turn down.

He was, after all, a patriot.

ABOUT THE AUTHORS

Jeremy Robinson is the international bestselling author of fifty novels and novellas including *MirrorWorld*, *Uprising*, *Island 731*, *SecondWorld*, the Jack Sigler thriller series, and *Project Nemesis*, the highest selling, original (non-licensed) kaiju novel of all time. He's known for mixing elements of science, history and mythology, which has earned him the #1 spot in Science Fiction and Action-Adventure, and secured him as the top creature feature author.

Robinson is also known as the bestselling horror writer, Jeremy Bishop, author of *The Sentinel* and the controversial novel, *Torment*. In 2015, he launched yet another pseudonym, Jeremiah Knight, for two post-apocalyptic Science Fiction series of novels. Robinson's works have been translated into thirteen languages.

His series of Jack Sigler / Chess Team thrillers, starting with *Pulse*, is in development as a film series, helmed by Jabbar Raisani, who earned an Emmy Award for his design work on HBO's *Game of Thrones*. Robinson's original kaiju character, Nemesis, is also being adapted into a comic book through publisher American Gothic Press in association with *Famous Monsters of Filmland*, with artwork and covers by renowned Godzilla artists Matt Frank and Bob Eggleton.

Born in Beverly, MA, Robinson now lives in New Hampshire with his wife and three children.

Visit Jeremy online at www.bewareofmonsters.com.

ABOUT THE AUTHORS

J. Kent Holloway is the author of six edge-of-your-seat paranormal thrillers and mysteries. A real-life paranormal investigator and 'Legend Tripper,' he explores the realms of myth, folklore and the unknown, in the southeast United States in his spare time. When not writing or scouring the globe for ghosts, cryptids and all manner of legends, he works as a forensic death investigator.

Visit him online at www.kenthollowayonline.com.

COMING IN 2016
FROM JEREMY ROBINSON

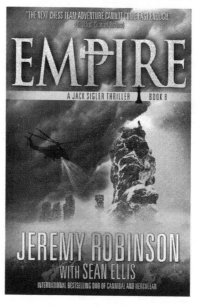

JACK SIGLER and the CHESS TEAM search
for his missing sister in
the next full-length adventure, *EMPIRE*.

To stay up to date on *EMPIRE* and other
releases, sign up for the newsletter at
www.bewareofmonsters.com.

Also Available
by J. Kent Holloway

The Dark Hollows...

Something sinister has awakened in a mysterious, dead patch of land in the foothills of the Appalachians...an evil that has been there long before the white man explored the primeval hills. And it has a hunger that must be sated.

Only one cursed man has the skill and knowledge to stop it. But to the people of Boone Creek, the enigmatic Ezekiel Crane might just be worse than the creature he's hell-bent on destroying.

Available at Amazon, BN.com, and wherever books are sold.